ADVENTURES WITH CAPTAIN MURPHY & LADY MURPHY

ADVENTURES WITH CAPTAIN MURPHY & LADY MURPHY

Written by Ernest R. Murphy

iUniverse, Inc.

New York Lincoln Shanghai

Adventures with Captain Murphy & Lady Murphy

iUniverse books may be ordered through booksellers or by contacting:

iUniverse
2021 Pine Lake Road, Suite 100
Lincoln, NE 68512
www.iuniverse.com
1-800-Authors (1-800-288-4677)

TXu 1-051-126

ISBN-13: 978-0-595-34019-4 (pbk)
ISBN-13: 978-0-595-78807-1 (ebk)
ISBN-10: 0-595-34019-9 (pbk)
ISBN-10: 0-595-78807-6 (ebk)

Printed in the United States of America

Introduction

The main theme of the book is the meeting of a man and a woman. The first section of the book has the unnamed main male character as the narrator. The second section of the book has the unnamed main female character as the narrator. The unnamed man character and unnamed woman character spend their time around Captain Murphy and Lady Murphy.

This book was written to provide wholesome and enjoyable reading for readers at various age levels. The characters, scenes, and locations have been clearly distinguished, though generally left unnamed, to allow the reader the privilege of visualizing their own setting.

Adventures with Captain Murphy

CHAPTER 1

The Coastal Setting

I had all the facts of a situation I had been thinking about for some time now. I tried to bring it together, yet it didn't quite seem to add up to any logical conclusion. I decided to pay a visit to my old friend, Captain Murphy.

He was unique in many ways. To a person who did not know him, he might have been mistaken for just another sea captain in charge of the sailors, known as "salts," who ran about the deck drawing up anchors, securing crates with hefty ropes, and hoisting the mainsail.

Captain Murphy's ship was a nice place to visit. There she sat in the harbor. The men onboard were masculine, mannerly, and in every way, gentlemen to the ladies.

I hurried over the brick-paved shopping square toward the ship. A runner board that ran from the ship to the dock, along with the strong ropes to hold her steady, let me know she had arrived to unload a fresh delivery of goods. As I rushed along, I was just nearing the bow of the ship when, out of the corner of my eye, I saw the most beautiful face I had ever seen. The lady turned and walked into the entrance of an inn.

My eyes still gazed toward the inn. The people inside looked out at me, and I at them. While I continued along, it was as though an invisible force grabbed me and pulled me off balance. I slipped and bumped against the railing of the pier that jutted out over the water.

I was making quite a spectacle of myself as I tried to regain my balance and composure. My eyes and mouth remained wide open with bewilderment, and my arms swung in a circular motion, in a futile attempt to grab hold of anything. I looked and sounded like a spooked chicken, right in front of everybody.

It was a safe and straight drop to the water below, and soon my head-over-heels descent began. As I fell, I could see the quick blur of snails and seaweed attached to the dock timbers. Taking a deep breath and covering my eyes, mouth, and nose, I prepared to hit the water below.

The fall was about ten feet down to the water, yet my embarrassment assured me the splash and noise was as though I had fallen one hundred feet. I went underwater, with the noise of air bubbles around me, and then rose up again. I was soon rising and falling with the tide like a cork on a fishing cane. My head was draped in seaweed, and my water-soaked hat was partly submerged about five feet away from me.

I could hear the sound of laughter and cheers above, from the ship and from the dock. What a blundering nut I had made of myself! As I dog-paddled over to my hat before it completely soaked through and sank, I heard a sailor's voice bellow from above, "Well, well, what have we here, a dissatisfied turtle, or a wharf rat?"

As if that wasn't enough, the sailor grabbed the bell-pull and clanged the bell, another sounded a horn, and yet another hollered unnecessarily, "Man overboard!" After that remark flew a doughnut-shaped lifesaver float. I grabbed the float and swam to the side of the ship opposite the dock and the inn, where I requested to be pulled up.

Once onboard, dripping, slipping, and then sitting down behind a large crate, I had to laugh about it myself. It would have been hilarious had I been watching it all. Recovering from the shock of the fall and the all-wet feeling, I suddenly thought of the beautiful face I had seen just before it all happened.

As drenched as I was, I was determined to peek at least from behind the crate to see if I could see her again. I didn't, and most of the onlookers were back to their business. I decided I was in no presentable fashion to make a first impression on a lady, especially since that impression would directly link me to such a blunder.

On the deck of the ship were bulky wooden crates and large burlap sacks with large letters spelling "COFFEE" and "TEA" on them, which assured me that the ship would remain in the harbor a few days. I knew this delivery would need to be unloaded here. This was a welcomed sight, because this meant another visit over a cup of coffee with Captain Murphy.

To my surprise, all the commotion had not brought Captain Murphy onto the deck. I then stood up and went around to inquire of the sailors where Captain Murphy was. They told me his whereabouts and pointed to the exchange quarters, where trade and transactions were confirmed for shipments.

Though I was anxious to see my old friend, who would have welcomed me despite my pitiful appearance, I did not want to chance another blunder of appearing before a beautiful lady while in such condition. I decided not to leave the ship and go to the exchange quarters where he was. The sailors gave me some fresh water to wash the sea sediments from my garments, showed me the shower so I could bathe, and gave me some clothes to wear temporarily until my hat and clothes dried.

The sun shining and a nice breeze blowing helped to dry my hat and clothes. I spent my time walking along the deck of the ship, tossing over to the sea gulls a few pieces of scrap shrimp and fish leftovers from the voyage. It was a way to pass the time. I watched the gulls as they swooped down in midair and caught their meal. Speaking of which, I thought a meal would be good soon. My own garments were clean and straight now, so I made myself as presentable as possible under the circumstances.

Some time had passed, and I heard a stir among the sailors. The sailors suddenly rose from their places, letting me know something had captured their attention. It was soon apparent Captain Murphy was on his way back to the ship. If everything followed the previous pattern, the sounds of the sailors calling back and forth would soon fill the air, along with the sounds of cranks, pulleys, hoists, and all the sounds of excitement of unloading the ship's cargo.

Captain Murphy walked onboard. With a quick smile and a hearty handshake, he then assumed a business-like manner, passing out invoices and receipts that itemized the freight and specified who was to receive each delivery. Much of the smaller freight shipments had already been unloaded, and the remaining crates were large orders for a few customers who had been in no real hurry to pick them up. Captain Murphy consulted his watch studiously to coordinate delivery times.

He had at his disposal a level to help determine the list of the ship, a mirror to signal to the hands on deck, and a magnifying glass. It was also very common for him to have available a telescope or pair of binoculars, and he usually had a pen and paper. In his pocket he sometimes carried his multipurpose knife. Occasionally, he would wear his captain hat or some other type of hat or cap.

He was unique in so many ways. Instrumentation, documentation, and observation were all part of his most distinctive traits. Although practicality would not always allow all of this equipment to be at his disposal, it was most preferred.

His personality and character were consistent, his habits religious, and his garments among the finest of clothes and sometimes among the beggarly of society. It was one of the greatest characteristics of his distinguished personality to be fair, just and understanding, regardless of a person's class in life. His firm discipline and adherence to his belief at times would place him at odds with others, but this did not produce compromise in him.

Soon along the dock appeared wagons and horse-drawn carriages. Captain Murphy had already settled the exchange at the exchange office, and the folks had come to pick up their goods. Captain Murphy turned to me and suggested a trip to the Captain's quarters. We left the sailors to busily distribute goods.

Captain Murphy could tell there was something on my mind that I desired to ask him. He questioned which dark corridor in the maze of life I was following. This was one of his ways of opening a conversation. He had a remarkable way of piecing loose ends together, so much so that it seemed he should have been an architect, engineer, or some great detective. He needed little information to arrive at the correct conclusion.

I once jokingly remarked to him that the first page of any book would tell him the whole story, and to read the rest of the book would only confirm what he already knew. He laughed. I told him about my incident of falling into the water and shared some of my thoughts with him. He and I then left the ship and went out onto the pier, where he resumed making a few calculations.

We then continued walking away from the ship. We were near an inn when I noticed a funny scene. "Look over there," I said. "There, by the trash can." For a while, Captain Murphy looked up and focused his attention in the direction I was pointing. He then walked to one side away from my view. I continued to watch the scene with delight as a large seafood-fattened sea gull rummaged through a nearby garbage can chained to a post. The bird intently pulled crumbs and scraps out of the can and proceeded to scatter the debris while he pecked at it for goodies.

Had no one noticed the sea gull doing this in plain view and in broad daylight, one would have easily suspected a large dog as the culprit. This bird seemed to have a positive attitude. He would drag a piece of garbage from the can, shake his head as if performing a dance, and then observe what fell out. After making a few selections, he would then start the process over again. It was funny to watch.

After watching the bird, I thought of the many great success stories in history. Cases where individuals rose from trash-heap situations of life's debris, against what seemed to be insurmountable odds, and with the help of God, do quite well for themselves. Some even acquired great fame and fortune, often to the benefit of society.

Even if success was against all known odds and was only the slightest chance, it was indeed a chance, and a chance of success in the right thing was worth pursuing. It was also true that there were many choices, multiple scenarios, dilemmas, and questions in life, as well as limited amounts of resources, such as time and money.

Although many people dream of being the greatest, the reality seems to be that a person should not chase every thought, expect to solve every mystery, close every business deal, gain every lady's heart, win every battle, and so on. The rational mind, therefore, would benefit to include both logical reasoning and faith, with a calm trust in providence.

During these thoughts, I observed that most of the outside dining tables at the inn were full of people. The various fishing boats used for catching lobster and shrimp were coming into port with their nets pulled up to dry. The boats were sitting lower in the water from the weight of their catch.

I had been caught up in my own thoughts, and only selectively noticing my surroundings. I then started to ask myself some questions while I refocused my attention. What time is it, and where is Captain Murphy? Captain Murphy…that's strange. It was not like him to just leave me without saying anything. I had lost sight of him.

Okay, let's see, I was standing here with Captain Murphy, and we were watching the sea gull ravage the trash can. What a hilarious sight. We both laughed. Anyway, it was about that time that Captain Murphy pulled his monocular telescope from his pocket and started to look around. I was doubled over with laughter, so much so, that I was no doubt becoming a spectacle to those around me who had no idea at what I was laughing.

About that time, I sat down on a bench nearby and continued watching the bird. I managed to get my laughter down to an inner chuckle. A few passersby, some being the most charming of ladies, looked at me half whimsically.

No doubt, they were wondering what in the world I had found so funny that I appeared as if I were some drunken person. The thought of being drunk or using mind-altering substances seemed so contrary to my belief of sensible reasoning and morality that I started to laugh again. I was absorbed in this episode.

Captain Murphy had begun walking in another direction and was making his way through the edge of the crowd. He was walking in and out of my view. I think it was around then I last saw him.

While I now tried to figure how I had lost sight of Captain Murphy, I almost became distracted. The crisp, cool, northeast air mixed with the right portion of warm sunshine, and produced an intoxicating effect in which I could certainly nap. But I wasn't going to nap right now. Where was Captain Murphy? Evening was almost here, and the boats were coming ashore, along with the tide.

CHAPTER 2

Events at the Inn

Straightening my hat and clothes a little, I proceeded to walk past the crowd. Visitors, vacationers, fishermen, and tradesmen gathered on the pier as I headed into one of the nearby eateries. At this moment, I needed something to tide over my appetite. I ordered a "small catch stew," which is a cup of clam chowder, and a glass of cranberry juice to go with it. I knew an opportunity for coffee was something I did not want to pass up, so I paid in advance and assured the chef I would return for it later. He gave me a token.

Gathering my cup of clam chowder and glass of cranberry juice, I walked over the creaking, sun-dried, unpainted wooden boards of the pier. I passed the sounds of muffled voices from a joyous and busy crowd of diners and workers as I continued toward the pier railing. I liked the crowd's gathering, but I also like the sea. Near the pier railing, I mastered an excellent view of both.

The tide had come in, and I could see the whitecaps in the distance. Near the pier, the water foamed as it rolled over the rocks, leaving seaweed and small shells attached. Every now and then, a moist ocean spray would cool the air. I heard the soothing rumble of the sea and the muffled voices of the crowd nearby. The smell of the salty sea and the smell of good food in the nearby eateries surrounded me.

While enjoying this scene, I prayed over my food and took my first bite. It was delicious and just the right temperature. I often preferred my food and beverage lukewarm.

I had done it again. I had certainly been daydreaming, or meditating, reflecting, or visualizing…whatever. It was peaceful to relax, and I had nowhere I just had to be right now. I took another sip of cranberry juice and another glance out to sea. How many ships had sailed the sea? What was it about the sea that intrigued people so much?

The lanterns around the pier were starting to cast their dim yellow light onto those who were gathered. Many of the dining tables were made of fine cast iron, with cushioned seats and an umbrella canopy. In the middle of the tables were white vanilla candles, which made them more elegant and attractive to couples. This provided a very romantic setting for those who might be courting sweethearts. Those tables were different from the mere crude wooden table where I comfortably sat.

Coffee! Time to get my cup of coffee! I got up from the seat, stretched my arms and legs a little, yawned, and waited for my eyes to get a little better adjusted before trying to move my way around the extended boots, high heels, petticoats, hats, and purses of those seated at the outside dining tables. Even the dining room inside the inn was packed full of customers getting coffee or tea. I waited in a short line of people and then finally made it to the counter.

I gave them my tray holding the empty dishes, produced my token, and was surprised and delighted at the size of the cup of coffee I received in return. Wow, fresh coffee, just into port! Wait a minute, I said to myself; this could be none other than a shipment from Captain Murphy himself. I took a few more sips…sure enough…it had to be.

I lingered for a short moment for the chance to ask the man behind the counter if the shipment and Captain Murphy had come into the inn at the same time, but the line had again lengthened with new customers. This inn dining room was a nice place and did a lot of business. I thought perhaps that I should start a similar inn of my own.

There was a fresh load of coffee just received into port. This was no doubt the coffee delivered by Captain Murphy. Captain Murphy was even occasionally referred to as Captain Coffee because he was the primary coffee provider.

That's it! That's where Captain Murphy had been during the time I was distracted by the sea gull. He had probably been overseeing the coffee shipment. That meant he might possibly still be around here. I walked away from the counter and casually glanced over the crowd, but there was no Captain Murphy in sight.

The next thing I knew, as physics and my taste buds would have it, I had emptied my cup of coffee, as large as it was. That was some good coffee, and, even though I planned to buy only one cup per day (if that much), this coffee was so good and so fresh, that I decided to purchase one more cup of the delicious stuff. My hand went into my pocket to gather up the necessary coins and back to the counter I went.

The line had dwindled, and one man was left purchasing his food. A lady and a man behind the counter took the orders. The man behind the counter nodded to me, and I knew I was next, but I paid him no attention. The lady behind the counter had caught my eye. I chose to wait in the line she was serving.

The man in front of me had received his food and turned to leave. I walked up to the counter and put down my money and empty cup. The lady smiled and asked me if I wanted a refill. I'm not sure how long I stood staring at her face, but I knew for a very short time that my heart seemed to flutter in step with her eyelids until it suddenly dropped into my boots. Her beautiful face was the one I had seen earlier before I had stumbled into the water. With all respect for her choices, I hoped she was not already married.

Either I was extremely tired, or my mind was playing tricks on me. I reasoned the whole room must have been full of peg-headed sailors who had been out all day glaring into the sun way too long if they had not noticed this lovely lady. Before I could think of the words to answer her, she had taken the cup to refill it with coffee.

While she was busy doing that, I checked my money stash to see if I could manage two meals at a nice candlelit table. She handed me the coffee, but I didn't leave the counter. I proceeded to ask who she was, if she was married, if she was hungry, what time she got off work, and so on.

She happened to be the daughter of the inn owner and was only helping, not a hired hand. She was single, ready for a break, and had no steady boyfriends. Had I gone too long without food, laughed too much earlier today, or been out in the weather too long myself? I thought luck like this only happens in imagination, not in real life.

Since her father was the inn owner, and she had helped him that day, the meals were free and in plentiful portions. We made our way around the musicians and out into the crowd. We picked a table that was private near the edge of the pier. It was still within the sound of the romantic music that the musicians provided. We ate our meals and talked for hours. We also promised to meet with each other again. We agreed this special moment was a delightful time that we hoped to always remember.

A couple near us left their table. It was then I caught a glimpse of…Captain Murphy! I couldn't believe it! No doubt he had been here for some time. That's all fine and dandy, I thought, but how long had he been here? That's what I wanted to know, but I didn't want to bother him by asking.

He was mostly private about his personal life and hardly ever mentioned it. In fact, right now, I didn't even want him to know I had seen him here. Obviously, it must not have been too private, since he was indeed in a public, though cozy, place, yet one where people minded their own matters. That's exactly what I decided to do.

My date pointed out another woman, and asked if I knew her, since I was looking toward that general direction. I was quick to explain that I had no interest in and had never before even seen the woman she was asking about. I reassured her that I was instead observing Captain Murphy and was surprised to see him here right now.

I let her know that Captain Murphy was my friend and that I had been visiting with him earlier today. I explained that I had lost sight of him in the crowd and did not know he was going to be here at the same time. I told her that I had searched to find him after I lost him, but that I had not seen him again until now.

In my own mind, I silently continued trying to figure out just how long Captain Murphy had been in this same area. I also tried to figure out how I had not noticed him earlier, even though I had only casually looked around to find him. I also wondered if he had already noticed that I was here with my lovely date.

The sound of my date's voice snapped my thoughts back to the present. I was somewhat aggravated at myself for being distracted from my present situation. A date like this was spectacular, and I was going to ruin it if I didn't watch out. Why should I concern myself with Captain Murphy right now? I wasn't going to take my voyage with him right now anyway.

My date and I finished our meals and continued talking. Slowly, we walked toward the edge of the pier railing. In her hand, she had brought along some of the pink rose petals that had been on the table where we had been sitting. As we talked, she cast them one by one, as if thoughtfully, out to sea. One often wonders what goes through a woman's mind, even while she talks openly. Perhaps it is just the curiosity of men, intrigued by such beautiful creatures of nature.

A waiter began gathering utensils from people that were finished with their meals. This, along with a small bell sounding and musicians packing up their instruments, was the polite way of letting everyone know they could continue visiting as long as they liked, but the inn dining room was soon closing for the night.

It was then that my date informed me she had promised earlier that day to help her father close the inn dining room. I offered to help them, but she preferred I did not. I was somewhat saddened by the fact that our conversation would end, but decided I was really expecting too much out of life, when, even after a very spectacular date, I was still disappointed it would soon end.

The walk back to the inn dining room doors was not that far from the pier railing, yet we took the longest route available and moved at a slow pace. We had just met, yet it seemed we had so many common interests. We continued our slow walk past the people still sitting at tables. We stood outside the inn dining room doors for some time until her father called for her. She said I could see her again at the inn dining room area and that it was a perfect meeting place. Though we dreaded the temporary departure, we exchanged good-byes and promised to meet again.

As soon as our glances disconnected and she closed the doors behind her, I spun on my heels and headed back out toward the tables on the pier. I nonchalantly, yet deliberately, headed over to where I had seen Captain Murphy, with hopes of getting a better understanding of what his plans were. I wanted to get a closer look at the man he had been talking with to see if I had seen him before today. I was most certain I had not.

As I drew closer, I saw Captain Murphy sitting there at one of the wooden tables, drinking a cup of coffee, but the chair across from him was empty. What? How in the world had I missed seeing this person? Oh well, what fate! Perhaps the man had departed for only a short while and would soon return.

I decided I would approach Captain Murphy in the usual way, as a friend who needed no invitation when he was not preoccupied, and as though nothing was different from any other time. "How are you Captain Murphy? How are things going?" I asked.

"Oh, fine," he responded with no hint of the unusual, and without saying much more than that.

I studied his face for any hint, but he just sipped his coffee. He must have figured there was nothing about the matter he thought necessary to mention to me. Though he was not one I thought had any vices, such as gambling, it was virtually impossible to read his expressionless face when he wanted to conceal a matter. Yet he had a wealth of secret information with which, if he had not been a man of integrity, he could have blackmailed many people.

Perhaps I shouldn't have used a sinister analogy to describe him, for those things were so contrary to his true character. Once he was presented with information, it was as though it were locked in a vault or lost at sea. That trait, along with his character and integrity, was probably what had made him the friend and confidant of so many people.

CHAPTER 3

Strange Happenings

Captain Murphy was a man of acute observation, quickly weeding out unnecessary details and going straight to the heart of the matter. He was a rugged man of both land and sea, yet he was such a gentleman with much respect and courtesy to the ladies. He was always so kind to them. Children loved to visit with him, and he seemed to know just the right things to say both to befriend and instruct them. He was not like some other businessmen, because it seemed a child's interest stopped his world for a moment and little else mattered. He seemed so skillful with them.

He was, in some other ways, very private and kept matters to himself. I tried to always honor and respect his judgment about keeping any issue private. I was not too timid to ask about things that I was curious about, but I did not press the issue if he did not provide the revealing answers I wanted; I guess I just respected his privacy. It seems respect should at least be a rule for most relationships.

However, I could not often hide my own thoughts from him, even though I tried. I am not saying he could read a person's mind; yet it seemed he did not need much information to figure out a person's general thought pattern. Just like so many other things that seemed to be similar to open books for his reading, my face and mannerisms seemed no different.

"I figure you will make plans to see her again, if you have not already made such plans," he said. "She seems to be very special to you," he said, smiling. "It is unusual to find a lady that has the same feelings for you as you have for her, and one who is so in step with your habits and methods that it is as though they are you—or at least the other half of you."

I found this very interesting. Not that what he was saying was so unusual, but the very fact he was saying these things. It was not like him to make such comments about just any lady with whom he saw me; however, he may have been giving friendly commentary on the general subject rather than referring completely to this particular relationship. I couldn't tell for sure.

I wanted to ask Captain Murphy what the setting was like when he decided to ask his wife to marry him. Where was she from? Where had he met her? How long had he known her? I wanted to ask him the questions I pondered in my own mind, but I restrained myself because I was more focused on my own situation and because I wanted to wait and see what he might say next.

I wanted him to talk a little more about the subject, and he did just that. While he talked, almost as if he was looking back into his own past, I could tell this subject was indeed very significant to him. He did not speak much about his own situation, but instead continued to talk more about my situation.

He finished his cup of coffee and sat it down on the table. He then commented a little about the weather and about some things he needed to get done tomorrow morning. He asked if I was ready and would like to board with him because there was ample room and plenty of hammocks below the ship's deck.

This sounded marvelous to me at the time, for I was very sleepy. In fact, I had been sleepy most of the day, even though I had a nap earlier. Only the exciting events of meeting my date and the spectacular coffee and food had kept me going.

It was not far to Captain Murphy's ship, so we did not take a carriage. I noticed that something seemed a little different about Captain Murphy's actions tonight. He would walk very briskly at times and very slowly at others. Sometimes his head would be down toward the ground, and, at other times, he would be looking up and around him. I also observed that when he would slow his pace, he would almost stop altogether and look out to sea, as if scanning its surface against the moonlight.

It seemed to me he was pondering something in his mind, as well as listening for something. Then he crossed right in front of me in a casual, but more deliberate way, which I knew was not in a direct path to the ship. I supposed he had planned a longer stroll to the ship because there was some lengthier conversation better discussed while walking. I looked up as we rounded an old stone building with nets, rafts, and lobster traps nearby. They were chained to one another, as though they had been placed outside to dry or for display.

With barely enough moonlight and a faint yellow glow from a streetlamp, I was shocked when Captain Murphy stopped, walked over to a lobster trap, and began giving me a lecture of its use. I thought this to be a rather unusual occurrence, but I decided to play the role of a curious observer, ignorant of lobster traps or at least of the unique design of this lobster trap.

Knowing Captain Murphy as I did, I knew there had to be a reason for this strange event. Right then, a man in dark clothing rounded the same corner that we had rounded. Looking shocked, the man stopped, straightened his clothes a little, yawned, looked around casually, and then continued on, as if his hesitation were only natural.

After he had walked out of sight, Captain Murphy let me know he had seen this man shadowing us ever since we had first left the pier. Captain Murphy knew many, many people that came and left the port, for he did business there regularly. However, he did not know this man, nor seem to have any idea why he was following us.

I had not noticed him until now, yet Captain Murphy said the man had been shadowing him since he left the pier and had been around the pier most of the time Captain Murphy had been there. Was this just a lost visitor or wanderer following us, suspecting that perhaps we, by chance, would be going to the same destination he needed to go?

If so, and as late and as dark as it was, why would the man leave such to chance? Surely his pride would not have prevented him from admitting his need of direction. Yet he had not asked us for direction. He had certainly been headed further out toward the shipping docks. While I was still thinking on these things, the same man again passed the street we were on and was heading back into town the opposite way.

Captain Murphy raised his voice a little more and continued rambling about the unique benefits, structure, and design of these newest lobster traps. Although I find lobster traps interesting, this was going on too long and was becoming too much. I looked again at Captain Murphy who explained in much quieter tones to me that I could either go on toward the ship, or I could follow him in the direction of the stranger.

About that time, on the other street, came the night watchman making his usual rounds. Captain Murphy spoke to the watchman and waved but made no sign to involve him in the pursuit of the stranger. I was getting kind of tired, and this made little sense to me. But Captain Murphy hurried my decision to either go or not, and he was already walking discreetly to follow the stranger.

I was tired, but this new excitement, along with my bottle of cranberry juice, revived my energy. We followed the stranger for only a few blocks, keeping about one block behind him. He turned and went into the lodge. We stayed for a moment, and then Captain Murphy peered from a distance through the entrance to watch the man.

After seeing the stranger leave the counter and head toward another part of the lodge, Captain Murphy followed in behind him, stopped at the registration desk, and stood there a moment talking with the lodge attendant. I stayed back in order to keep watch from outside.

Captain Murphy did not stay very long and soon returned to where I was. As it turned out, the stranger had not left his name. However, Captain Murphy said the attendant had mentioned the stranger was an investigator from overseas called in to assist the local police. We then left the lodge and headed back toward the ship.

As we passed some shops, Captain Murphy mumbled to himself with seeming satisfaction, something about "so they have arrived." I assumed this was his reference to an expected shipment. I was ready to sleep, since I felt that his concerns, whatever they had been and for whatever reason they were about, were answered, and everything was all right.

We wasted no time in our pace to Captain Murphy's ship. The loading ramp, which had extended from his ship to the dock, was no longer there, having been drawn back onboard. Ropes, however, still extended snuggly from the bow and near the stern of the ship. The ship's rigging and sails lay nearby so as not to catch wind.

However, I noticed few of the moorings secured, as they had been earlier. This struck me as somewhat unusual. I knew of no reason for it to be this way, since, to my knowledge, Captain Murphy was not intending to set sail for a while. Again, this unusual circumstance appeared to present no alarm to Captain Murphy, and so I brushed the issue aside as irrelevant.

The ship was dimly lit with lanterns. When we boarded, there were only a few sailors above board, shuffling a few items here and there, and a few were playing a game. No money or anything like that was involved, but they were exclaiming words like, "I bet you can't top this score."

As we went below deck, the wooden stairs creaked beneath our steps. The ship moved only gently with the water underneath its hull. A very calm night at sea it must be, for if it had continued to be a strong tide as it had been earlier, the ship would be swaying more than it was, even with all of the moorings secured.

As we walked, Captain Murphy pointed to a number of wooden kegs standing upright that were held together with metal strips. One had a hand pump on top of it and a pan underneath. With this, a nearby cup could be filled with fresh drinking water. I poured a cup.

Toward the back part of the ship was a built-in shower. It was unique. This was one of the neatest showers I had ever seen, and Captain Murphy had designed it himself. On the top deck, kegs were used to catch fresh rainwater or they were filled with fresh water from the port well. Water flowed from one of the large kegs, through an iron pipe that crossed over a furnace. The pipe ran to a nozzle, which could be turned on in the shower below.

During the coldest months, the sailors would take turns heating the furnace and taking showers. It was an ingenious method of providing warm showers. A small stepladder near the shower entrance was used to get into the shower. This was needed because a tub surrounded the bottom portion of the shower and helped to prevent any overflow.

The drain had a pipe that sloped downward and ran to the outside of the hull. The entire shower was positioned a little higher in order to allow gravity enough distance to drain the used water out to sea. I wanted a shower, even though I was tired.

Captain Murphy went about his somewhat usual routine of looking over the ship chart times and merchandise log. After that, his common practice was reading Scripture and retiring to sleep.

It was not my first time onboard, so I just grabbed a towel and washrag from the rack and took my shower. I noticed as I came out of the shower that there was a room nearby, or so it seemed it could be a room. When I voyaged on this ship before, I always ignored that room, believing it to be just a storage closet. I never even bothered to inquire about it nor look into it.

Even though I did not stop and check it out tonight, I wondered if it were a room rather than just a storage closet. It was located in the stern end of the ship, and I could still see it from my hammock, which was not very far away.

CHAPTER 4

Lively Occurrences

I lay down and said my prayers as usual before I drifted off to sleep and started to dream. During my dream, I thought I heard a very low sound of music coming from that room near the shower. It surprised me that the other sailors did not hear the sound. Perhaps they made voyages so often that they were used to it and just blocked it out.

The noises from that room sounded like voices mixed with music. There seemed to be a gleam of light coming from under the door. I got up, walked over to the door, and placed my ear against it. Sure enough, I heard music and voices. I knocked on the door and was welcomed in to the inn dining room by my date's father. I then saw my lovely date again.

She did not hesitate to bring out coffee to me. She knew I loved coffee. I reasoned that I really could use coffee right then, for I still felt a little bit sleepy. In my groggy mindset, my coordination was off, and my hand bumped the coffee cup instead of grasping it, sending the coffee flying all over the counter—but luckily not on anybody. I jumped to clean it up…and realized only then that I had been dreaming.

I rolled over to go back to sleep, but I heard a very low humming sound again. Instead of music, it was a sound similar to that of gears, pulleys, and levers. My eyes were turned away from that room, and I thought I could put this entire episode aside until early tomorrow morning.

There it was again: a low hum of gears, or pulleys, or something like that. It had to be. I made sure I wasn't dreaming this time and looked toward the room, certain that this was where the sounds were coming from. Along with a very dimly lit lantern, which provided little light, there was indeed a light coming from under the door of that room.

I was still partly asleep as I squinted with my eyes. I quickly glanced around the ship's interior. The hatches were pulled shut, and all of the portholes tightly closed. The ship was rocking, so we must have surely encountered a storm. The hull tossed from side to side, and the bow of the ship rose and then the stern—not in an extreme way, but much more than desired when docked in port.

Wow, somebody had better tie the moorings, or the ship will be broken up right here against the pier! What an embarrassment and what danger! I jumped from my hammock and hollered out to the others still sleeping. We had to get the ship secured to the large timbers and rocks in the port, or we would lose the ship against it.

The ship rocked suddenly, and immediately the door to the storage room, or whatever kind of room it was, swung open, exposing additional light, and then quickly shut again. Rushing toward me was one of Captain Murphy's sailors. He approached me so fast I thought he would run right over me.

It seemed he was not going forward to secure the ship. He instead hurried toward me with his hand to his mouth as if signaling me to be quiet. I was startled and puzzled at the same time. If this man was awake during all of this, why hadn't he woken up the rest of us so the ship could be saved? Was he a traitor? Did he want the ship to crash?

Just then another one of Captain Murphy's sailors rushed down from above deck. He was dressed in all black. I wondered to myself what in the world was going on. This was too much. I had just turned around to face this other sailor and started to say something, when all of a sudden the sailor behind me told me to keep quiet.

To my surprise, this other sailor also rushed toward me with his hand to his mouth, as if to signal me to be quiet. I was very confused and puzzled about all of this. The sailors then said they were watching something and I had to be quiet. The other men in their hammocks were awake and had turned over to see the commotion. The two sailors quickly quieted them, but the others seemed to suspect something unusual was going on.

But what about the ship? Was it being secured? Was there a storm? Why were Captain Murphy and some of the sailors awake? Why did everybody have to be so quiet? In a storm, sailors very often holler back and forth things like, "hold her steady," "batten down the hatches," "secure the lines," and so on. Just then, another sailor motioned to the two sailors near me. They quietly rushed upstairs.

I rushed to change out of my sleeping clothes into my regular ones. I also grabbed my raincoat, hat, and boots and clumped my way up the ladder. I at least managed to get a look above deck, even though I had not left the ladder yet. Just as I was near the top rung of the ladder, one of the sailors, dressed in very dark clothing, saw the top of my bright yellow rain cap and hurried over to keep me below deck. He was not slipping or sliding on a rain-soaked deck, nor was he dressed in rain clothes. He wasn't even wet from a storm.

The deck of the ship also wasn't wet. There was no thunder, no lightning, and no crashing waves. The moon was in reasonably clear view. I was confused. In a hushed voice, the sailor asked what in the world I was doing and why I was dressed up like that. He then refused to let me climb any further up the ladder and told me to go below deck, and he would quickly explain. I did as he said, and he followed quickly after me.

He told me we were at sea right now and no longer at port. At sea! Why were we at sea? Captain Murphy had said nothing about this. The sailor filled me in on some more details, letting me know he didn't have all of them, but that right now we were probably less than one mile out at sea and traveling at the speed of only about two knots. We were looking for a white ship, and this all had something to do with a man Captain Murphy had noticed following him at the pier last night.

It was already early morning, but only about thirty minutes after midnight. The sailor continued to tell me the hatches were pulled shut and all of the portholes covered so no light could be seen by the other ship. Anyone who came above deck had to wear dark clothing only, so there would not be the slightest chance of the moon or the stars casting enough light on them that they would be noticed.

No man on board had the unacceptable habit of smoking, so there was no chance of a flame being lit, not even for the stove, at this particular time. What was all this secrecy about? What was the importance of it all, and why did we have to be so quiet, even below deck? The sailor again told me he didn't know all of the details, but he knew everybody was being quiet so we wouldn't be noticed by the other ship passing nearby.

Wasn't this very risky business, I asked, since Captain Murphy's ship was solid flat black? The sailor agreed this was very risky business, for the two ships could collide at night, not seeing each other in the darkness. However, there was a plan in place to prevent such an accident. The sailor then said he needed to go above deck again in case they needed him. He said I could follow, but not to wear the noisy rain boots or the bright yellow rain clothes!

I changed into some dark clothes. This was exciting, yet, at the same time, I still did not know for sure what was going on. It was evidently not an absolute emergency, for all the sailors would be out of their hammocks and busy. However, this was evidently very important for some reason, because it was being done with much secrecy. I put on one more boot and tightened my belt, and I was on my way above deck. As I walked, I wondered if I would be able to see what all the commotion was about in the dark.

Okay, here goes: over to the ladder, up the ladder, and above deck. To my shock and surprise, there was no one to be seen! This was just too much! The deck was almost pitch black, except for the few traces of moonlight that lit up certain areas of it. For a moment, I again thought it must somehow all just be in my mind…nothing but a dream. I quickly swept that thought aside. This was not a dream.

I did not know which direction to look in, but I knew I had to be very careful. No bumping into things and making loud noises, no hollering out asking where everybody was, and no careless steps like I had made at the port. The sea was much deeper out here, and the surroundings much darker. It would be a lot harder to rescue me this time. Besides, this was a very important mission, and it required seriousness and attention to detail. I certainly wanted to do my part to make it a success. Because I knew Captain Murphy, I trusted this mission was not for any bad or mischievous purpose on our part.

Amid all of the excitement and mystery, I was somewhat awestruck by the magnificence around me. This was the work of God. The moon, the stars, the vast ocean of water, and the darkness surrounding me all had order and unity that held it all together in harmony.

What a magnificent and masterful mind it had to be: omniscient, omnipotent, and omnipresent. There was no place in the world, at any time, I could be that He, the Creator, was not and did not know what was going on in my life. The King James Version of the Bible says in Isaiah 9:6, in reference to Jesus: "Wonderful, Counsellor, The mighty God, The everlasting Father, The Prince of Peace." Also, the Scriptures in Matthew 1:21–23 refer to Jesus as "God with us." The Scriptures in John 1:3–4 state, "All things were made by him; and without him was not any thing made that was made. In him was life; and the life was the light of men."

This was all so magnificent. I supposed that it was at least partly true that people could sometimes be more aware of God's presence when they were humbled by some overwhelming or magnificent circumstance of life. It was occasionally in those moments of humility that their human spirit properly acknowledged God as supreme and their need of God.

My thoughts reminded me of the story in II Corinthians 12:10 about the Apostle Paul, who also sailed and who had been a relatively frequent traveler. "For when I am weak, then am I strong," he said. Writings concerning him seemed to indicate that he was a very strong-willed man, highly educated, and determined in what he believed. He had been a traveler by both land and sea. He had endured false accusations and had even been wrongly put in jail. As a traveler by sea, he had been shipwrecked numerous times, yet he indicated he was at his best when he totally yielded to God.

I said to myself, "God, help me to yield to You and to Your will." This I had to do. I was determined to continue reading Scriptures and searching for God's will in my life. Though I could not compare myself with the Apostle Paul, except maybe in his traveling. (I do remember reading Scriptures about his Damascus Road experience and his sea voyages, which, in some ways, were really not that much different from my own.)

Although I sometimes pray aloud, this time I prayed very quietly. A new light of understanding had brightened me inside. I knew this was just a small part and not all that God had planned for me.

Just like the Apostle Paul, no matter where in the world I was, or how dark the surroundings might be, I would strive to continue to obey God and let God's light shine and guide my path. I knew this knowledge was what everyone needed, yet could not find in any travel or anything else. This knowledge was heavenly and could not be obtained by mere earthly means.

CHAPTER 5

Who Catches Whom?

I wanted action…or so I thought. Everything was so quiet. For all I knew, a spider could have been weaving a web in my hair right now. I knew I would have to be quiet in doing so, but I decided I was going to move from where I was. I knew there were others on the deck of the ship, and I was going to get around and find somebody…anybody. They must have all been hiding or something.

I decided I would stay on my hands and knees and crawl my way around the ship. I didn't want to make noise, run into anything, or lose my balance. It was hard to tell how much farther we had gone out to sea, for I did not readily have an instrument with which to sight in on the stars and calculate our precise geographical location.

I did not feel a strong wind, but it did seem the waves were a little larger, though not bad. This suggested we were probably still moving a little farther out. I tried to guess our location by the position of the moon, but its position changes throughout the night. It seemed like it wasn't really that much later. It was probably only about one or one-thirty in the morning.

I had crawled only about eight feet or so when I heard someone whisper, "Do you see that?"

It was Captain Murphy!

"See what?" I whispered.

"There—in the moonlight," he said. He took my arm and extended it in the direction I should look.

I looked intently into the darkness, allowing my eyes to adjust and gather any bit of light they could. I did see something. The longer I focused, the clearer the image became. It was a white ship. Above it, though, I could not make out any masts or sails. I questioned Captain Murphy if some paddle propelled this mysterious ship, since there were no sails showing and yet it was moving.

Captain Murphy explained that, from knowledge he had gathered earlier, this was possibly a cargo ship, and that it was only powered by sails in the wind. The hull was white, but the masts, moorings, and sails were all black. The reason behind this was supposedly to avoid detection at night. The hull sat low in the water, possibly due to the weight of some cargo.

This mysterious ship could easily be mistaken as a "whitecap" of a wave, which was common at sea. The dark masts and sail riggings would, at a distance, either not be seen or blend in with the darkness. Even if noticed against moonlight, the sails could be mistaken as merely a dark cloud, heavy fog, or some other illusion, especially to a sleepy or casual observer.

How then, I wondered, did Captain Murphy even know of this ship—about it, or its course? I asked Captain Murphy that very thing. At that time, Captain Murphy had very little detail about the ship, but figured the vessel was capable of carrying cargo. He said he knew of these things from information gathered by the lighthouse keeper stationed near the port. The lighthouse keeper had been notified earlier by Captain Murphy and port authorities to continue watching for any unusual or mysterious vessels. The keeper was to signal if he saw anything suspicious.

A sailor made his way past me and headed to the hatch to go below deck. I followed him. This sailor went straight toward the storage room, where earlier I had seen the light shining from underneath the door. The sailor went right in, and I followed. There were already three sailors in the room. One sailor was pouring oil, the other sailor was tightening a valve with a wrench, and the last sailor was checking the pulley belts and gauges.

This was an awesome engine of some sort! I wasn't sure what type, what horsepower, or how it was powered, but I noticed the belts, pulleys, levers, and gears attached centrally to iron axles. Oh my! I was excited like a kid in a toy factory. I loved this kind of stuff. I was absolutely fascinated by machinery and engines and by things such as pendulum clocks. I could not tell what was powering this engine, yet it was running and was very quiet.

I started to hear the combined low rumble of the engine and the propellers stirring the water underneath our ship's stern. It seemed our concern now was to travel fast in order to catch the other ship, or get away from it, or whatever it was we were trying to do. What were we planning to do? Captain Murphy no doubt had a plan, but I sure didn't know what it was.

Maybe this motor, whatever type it was, was more efficient than I realized. I turned around to comment about this to one of the sailors, but they had already left the room. I wanted to stay there and see the motor run. Instead, I hurried to find Captain Murphy. I immediately went above deck, and there he was, along with some other sailors, in the darkness.

They were hurriedly repositioning the midnight blue sails, which were Captain Murphy's selected color. This would help our speed and would serve as night camouflage. With our ship empty of all its freight, it was "full speed ahead." This, along with the design of the hull, made sailing a speedy voyage.

We were gaining on the other ship, even though we had altered our course of pursuit to avoid being caught in any moonlight reflection on the water and being seen by anyone on the enemy ship. The enemy ship! What was I saying? I had no confirmation that this was an enemy ship.

I suppose my own questions about the mystery and adventure of it all had also led me to think that because this was some mystery ship that I didn't fully understand, it must be involved in something bad. It might have been fun to pretend I was in a contest against the skills and abilities of the sailors on the other ship, but this shouldn't cause me to think badly of them just because I didn't understand them or know what they were doing.

For all it mattered, I did not even really understand what I was doing, or what Captain Murphy and his crew were doing, or what any of us on either ship was doing at this hour of the morning, racing through darkness in deep sea waters. This was, I guess, what people referred to as blind trust—confidence—and I had confidence in Captain Murphy.

We were only a little ways from the port. The white ship was headed straight into the port where we had been earlier. The lanterns near the port remained partly lit for the unloading of ships, in case a delay prevented a ship's arrival before evening and was then required to unload during the night.

Well, if this was all it was, then what was the big deal? However, it stood to reason that even if this ship and its sailors were not up to some sinister matter, it was still a little mysterious, especially with all of the secrecy surrounding it.

We slowed our pace and watched from sea until the white ship had docked and then secured its moorings to the pier timbers. To my surprise, Captain Murphy then ordered that our ship be taken immediately into port.

The white ship let down its ramp, and then the sailors started to unload its cargo. After only a small portion of the cargo had been moved down the ramp and stacked on the dock, a group of four wagons drawn with teams of horses came out of the darkness and pulled near the edge of the dock.

At the same time, Captain Murphy blocked the white ship in by ordering his sailors to rope the stern of our ship to one end of the pier and the bow to the other end of the pier timbers. This closed off the small channel where the white ship was located.

Near the very top of the tall center mast of our ship, I noticed two lanterns had been lit and were hanging there, burning brightly. No doubt, the night watchman would see this from a church steeple nearby. Captain Murphy and some of his men hurriedly exited the ship, and I followed.

Captain Murphy had just taken a few steps forward, with me beside him, when I noticed someone stepping out of the darkness a little way in front of us. The man was moving quickly, and, as he approached, it became obvious this was the stranger that had followed Captain Murphy and me yesterday from the pier. It seemed to me that Captain Murphy had at least seen the stranger.

The stranger said, "Looks like we've caught him this time."

What…Caught Captain Murphy?

Two other men approached from the darkness. I was alarmed. We thought we had blocked them in, but they had led Captain Murphy into a trap. Why were they doing this? What had he done to deserve this?

Just then, Captain Murphy quickly shook hands with the stranger, and I then understood they were talking about finally catching someone on the other ship, rather than catching Captain Murphy. Captain Murphy, his men, the stranger, and I all walked hurriedly toward the white ship.

So this was it! The people on the white ship were smuggling something into the port. The man receiving the shipment was the owner of the store where the lobster traps were—where Captain Murphy and I had stopped the night before when the stranger came by.

The police were there at the scene, but there weren't any arrests being made and no demonstrative force being used. Perhaps the police felt they had all of the evidence they needed and that the criminals would not abandon all of their possessions and leave with their ship. Captain Murphy stepped forward to speak with the night officer standing near the bottom of the white ship's loading ramp. The officer and Captain Murphy then walked up the ramp.

Another man stepped out onto the deck, obviously the captain of the other ship. My adrenaline was flowing. I felt ready to snap into action, but I had no real handle on what was going on there. To my surprise, the sailors from the white ship were allowed to continue delivering the lobster traps. Obviously, there was no reason to be alarmed.

This had been exciting, and still was, but I wanted at least an answer for all of the commotion. Just then, Captain Murphy, the police officer, and the captain of the white ship shook hands. Captain Murphy turned around and headed back down to where I was. Then he looked around again and waved to the captain of the other ship, who also waved back. The lobster traps were still being unloaded, and the police officers were returning to their posts.

Captain Murphy came to me, half chuckling and shaking his head. What a continual turn of events this day had been, and what an unusual night! It seemed everybody was one big peaceful community now—for whatever reason—although that is a favorable way for things to be.

Some of Captain Murphy's crew had already returned to his ship. It seemed as though a good night of sleep might remedy the whole situation. Captain Murphy placed his hand on the back of my shoulder, and we continued walking with the others toward his ship.

As we walked, he briefly said to me that everything was okay and just about over with. He said that he would explain it all in detail after some rest, unless I wanted to stay up even longer and hear it all right now. I suggested to him that it would all sound better and make more sense after I rested, especially while I was having a nice cup of coffee later in the morning.

Soon we were back onboard Captain Murphy's ship. The sailors untied it and allowed it to float gently away from the port, while they used long oars to prod and push it away from the edge of the pier. The white ship was pulling its ramp in and, in just a few minutes, would be moving out of the channel and docking alongside the port until daybreak. We also docked alongside the port.

I was glad to get back to our ship, for I was really tired. Nevertheless, the adventure had been great for the excitement. I went below deck, changed into my sleeping clothes, and climbed into my hammock. I looked over toward the room where the engine was. A light was still shining from under the closed door. I decided it would be interesting to find out more about that engine later on, but for now, I was ready to go to sleep.

CHAPTER 6

More Questions than Answers

I woke up the next morning when the ship's bell sounded. Around me there were beams of sunlight coming in through the portholes. I must have missed the first bells that sounded and slept right through them. From the position of the sunshine on the floor, it had to be around nine in the morning. I had slept late, and that was good.

Good sleep from the night before would help the day go better. I got up, stretched my arms and legs, and walked over to the washbasin. I brushed my teeth and then tried to get my hair to look half decent. From my view in the mirror, it looked like an irritated porcupine, a windblown rooster, or an ostrich with a bad hairdo! It was a mess! I wet and combed it, slapped my hat on it, and made my way for breakfast above deck on the ship.

I inquired where Captain Murphy was and found out he was above deck with some of his crew. I went above deck to join them. They had just about emptied the large coffeepot sitting near them. They had fresh bread from the bakery. We had plenty of coffee to grind. Coffee was one of the commodities Captain Murphy had delivered. I scooped up some coffee beans, put them in the grinder, and wound the crank.

I went over to the metal coffeepot sitting on the burner. I unlatched the small lever that loosened the holding band around its top—which kept it from turning over during sailing. Removing the old grounds, I put the fresh ground coffee in the metal strainer. Opening the stove door, I placed a few more coals inside, and, in no time, the sea air was mixed with the smell of freshly brewed coffee. The aroma of freshly brewed coffee smelled as good as any candle or lady's perfume…well, maybe not!

The sound of laughter and muffled conversation in the background continued and brought my thoughts back to the activity around me. I couldn't believe it. Two sailors were already engrossed in a game, determined to outdo the other this time and beat their previous score.

I pulled one of the thick ceramic coffee mugs from the cupboard. This was my favorite type of coffee mug. I turned the valve on the spout of the coffeepot and filled my mug half full. Filling the mug half full was a trick I had learned to avoid spilling my drink. I sat down on a nearby crate and listened in on the varying dialects and conversations buzzing about. Finally, I asked Captain Murphy about the previous night's adventure.

Captain Murphy began to unfold the mystery. He began by saying, "It is routine procedure for the police watchmen to monitor the port. A few months ago, the lighthouse keeper noticed a suspicious looking ship passing by the lighthouse.

"The ship was noticed in the evening a short distance from the port when the lighthouse light shown upon it. The ship seemed to be steered, and did not float as though it was abandoned, yet there was no sign of lights or crew noticed onboard. The lighthouse keeper thought the ship seemed somewhat suspicious looking.

"The lighthouse keeper, therefore, dispatched his boat the next day, and it was reported to the local port authorities. The description of the ship was not clear enough to completely verify the ship's identity, and no ship matching the vague description had made documented delivery into this port any time recently. The ship was unknown to authorities, just like the ship last night and early this morning, so it raised suspicion.

"The port authorities, knowing the speed of my ship and her solid black appearance, solicited my help in pursuit of this 'mystery ship.' We communicated to the lighthouse keeper to be on the lookout for any other suspicious vessels or activity.

"The local port authorities, which were informed of recent suspicious activities in various ports in other countries, notified some detectives from overseas and requested they also assist in the matter. This is why the stranger that followed us last night was here. I was not sure the stranger we saw was one of the detectives from overseas until I followed him and asked the attendant at the nearby lodge.

"Only then was I sure of it. Until that time, I had to assume this man might be part of the wrong side of the suspicious activity. He had been watching me, and I had been watching him and anyone he associated with, for I suspected he wasn't acting alone, regardless of which side he was on. I was surprised when I saw him talking to the inn owner's daughter who had brought coffee to his table."

When Captain Murphy mentioned that the inn owner's daughter had been talking with this stranger, my heart fell to my boots, but this time I felt a little let down. Why did she care about this stranger? I understood at least one reason why he would be talking to the inn owner's daughter. She was absolutely gorgeous. I guess, in some ways, I could at least understand her interest in him, for he was a clean-shaven man, strongly built, and well-dressed. None of that mattered to me. It just didn't seem right, no matter how reasonable it was, that she would really fall for this other man.

Captain Murphy, as if reading my thoughts, continued. "I knew this might bother you about the young lady involved, but, at that time, secrecy was important, and she had to be under surveillance also, even though she was the local inn owner's daughter. The shop owner who had the lobster traps was also under surveillance for recent and frequent late night trips alone.

"I was notified that some strange events were taking place and were being investigated by the authorities. I was asked to help by monitoring all activity that might be related in anyway. I felt awkward—especially monitoring the shop owner I had known and done business with for years. In my heart, I felt all would be okay as soon as the facts were gathered. As it turned out, the inn owner's daughter is also a detective."

When Captain Murphy said that, I was so shocked, I almost spilled my coffee. A detective! She was too pretty and too ladylike to be a detective. I was also excited by the fact that detectives from overseas were on this very case. Captain Murphy chuckled. I knew this was not the first time he had assisted with the law enforcement.

As the story unfolded, I began to wonder if knowing these new facts only presented a bigger mystery instead of explaining the previous mystery. My mind was intrigued by it all. The more answers I didn't have, the more questions I had.

Captain Murphy continued. "I noticed the inn owner's daughter was around the inn dining area a lot more lately. The inn owner said she had just recently returned from visiting her aunt who lives overseas. She has been staying with her parents lately. The stranger we followed was from overseas, as were two other men he brought with him. All three men were detectives and had recently journeyed here on a large ship of travelers.

"The local authorities checked their port logs with those at the exchange quarters to verify any records of previous shipments from abroad to the lobster trap shop owner. Some while back, a local plainclothes police officer asked the owner if or when a new shipment of lobster traps was due and was able to determine a more specific date when a shipment of any kind might arrive.

"A new shipment was due into port today or the following day. Since this was a much later date, local officials had plenty of time to be prepared and even call for the assistance of detectives from overseas. The lighthouse keeper had been notified to be particularly watchful these last few nights and to signal if anything unusual occurred. It did, and the lighthouse watchmen spotted the 'mystery ship' just over on the other side of the lighthouse.

"He then made the secret light signal to the port night watchmen stationed in the church tower steeple. I was then notified, and we immediately set out to sea around midnight in order to make the port seem rather empty of activity. That, as you know now, resulted in our midnight voyage, and our event of blocking the other ship in the port channel.

"While we were docking, the police were already investigating the delivery of the other ship's cargo, which turned out to be predominantly lobster traps, and which showed nothing really suspicious at all. However, being thorough, more search and inquiry was made. Then I thought for sure I recognized this ship's captain as a friend of mine.

"I then went onboard with an officer to meet the captain of the other vessel. Sure enough, he was an old friend I had not seen for some time. He was always a realist and took joy in disproving questionable tales and mysterious events. As it turned out, someone had challenged him.

"They told him that if he would dare to cross under certain stars around the rocks of the old lighthouse and then head toward the port, he would find gold. The gold from an old pirate ship full of gold, which sank after hitting the rocks near where the lighthouse now stands, would reflect a beam from the stars and show the gold's exact location. All of this, of course, would make the crew that found it extremely rich.

"Even with the lighthouse now standing nearby, part of the tale says that the gold is near the home of a mysterious sea dragon in those waters. Some have even said the sea dragon might have distracted the original crew of the pirate ship to the point it caused them to damage the hull of their ship on the nearby rocks and sink.

"My friend, the captain of the ship we followed, having charts of the course around the rocks, had taken the challenge of this old tale to prove it wrong and put it to rest. His ship was always white, and the sails of it were always black, and so there was really nothing unusual about that. The purpose of having all of the lamps out, at least during the time under the particular stars of that course, was to further dispel the tale.

"It has been said that if there were lights onboard, the reflection from the gold on the pirate ship would only blend with the lights of a ship's lanterns. Then the gold would never be seen. It also has been said that the lights would prevent a person's eyes from seeing the faint glimmer of the starlight beam reflected from the gold.

"My friend, the captain of the white ship, is scientific and methodical like myself. He never believed the tale, but he liked to take challenges. Since he needed to make a delivery into the port here anyway, he determined he would disprove the tale all together. Attempting to disprove the tale a couple of times within recent months resulted in his somewhat suspicious activity near here and the lighthouse.

"However, the story of the sunken pirate ship loaded with gold is still believed to be real. Although the exact location of the wreck is not precisely known, it is believed that a pirate ship did sink near the deep waters around the lighthouse, but it has never really been proven."

The story Captain Murphy told proved to be so interesting that I had not gotten up, even one time, to get coffee while he was telling it. The story about the sunken treasure ship sounded like another mystery, since there were reports of a sunken pirate ship with no known survivors that had crashed near the lighthouse.

I sat there enjoying the nice view and pondering the most recent events that had taken place. Though Captain Murphy had explained the night's adventure, I was still trying to adjust to the matter. It was a lot to absorb in such a short time. In this conversation, I had found out that my date was a detective. I wondered if she were really interested in me, or if I was just part of her case.

There had also been the pursuit of the ship in the dark of night. Now there was this new development about the story of sunken treasure. Even though I had what seemed to be many pieces of a puzzle, and I knew how some of them fit together, it would still take some more time for me to assimilate it all.

CHAPTER 7

The Secret Plans

The ship's bell sounded. It was near mealtime, and people were already gathering at the local eateries. I wanted to visit someone there. I made myself as presentable as possible. I had a few mixed emotions right now, but I determined I would not let these emotions prevent me from seeing my date, the gorgeous daughter of the local inn owner.

Besides, even if she was a detective and had been talking with some other man, she was still single and had the right to talk to whomever she wanted. In fact, for all I knew, I might be considered the "other man" to someone she was dating before me. I went below deck and made sure that I looked my best before going over to the inn dining room.

As usual around mealtime, the tables on the pier were loaded with people visiting and having meals, and the port was busy with the regular run of the fish and shrimp boats in and out of port. I entered the inn dining room.

There she was, behind the counter, but she was not waiting on people at the counter. She turned and walked out of sight to what I guessed was the kitchen area. It seemed she did this as soon as she had seen me.

When I approached the counter to place an order, I spoke to her father. I thought for a moment I had lost out, and though I was hungry, I only ordered a glass of tea. I wished I had not even come in, for I was afraid she had changed her mind about seeing me.

Just then, her father convinced me to go out to a reserved table with an umbrella over it, which sat next to the pier edge, near the best view of the ocean. He said his daughter would bring out my tea to me in just a moment. I figured I would at least get a chance to talk everything over with her.

I was surprised when I reached the reserved table, and she brought out a meal. Most of all, there she was, as pretty and as kind as ever. We talked and exchanged more information about ourselves, about our interests, and about our goals in life. We also talked at length about some of the most recent developments and what they meant in regards to our relationship.

She assured me that my concerns about another man were unfounded. I was relieved to know that none of the previous events or issues had changed our feelings for one another. We talked about how we felt for each other and how it all seemed so different together than it did with anyone either of us had met before.

We promised we would try to meet again and try to keep in touch somehow, regardless of where in the world we might be and no matter how far apart we might find ourselves from one another. We also promised we would try to have some means of communication, regardless of how things turned out; but it seemed we both realized our hearts were more involved with one another than that.

The fact we cared so much about each other was true, and nothing could ever change that. We would see each other again, Lord willing. That was our promise.

It was around three in the afternoon, but it seemed that the time had passed so fast. Having unfinished business to tend to overseas, she had to return aboard the ship she had arrived on a few days earlier. Her parents and I helped her with her belongings.

I watched through Captain Murphy's binoculars until the ship was out of sight. Her ship was leaving, but somehow it seemed like my ship had come in, as the saying goes. Our hearts were anchored together, and nothing would ever change that. Before I turned to go and load some freight onto Captain Murphy's ship, I had to assure myself again: this was more than just a dream.

She said she would return to this very port within a few months and that we could meet here again. Meanwhile, we would write and try to send messages through Captain Murphy or others that would be traveling. Captain Murphy's ship would be leaving on a journey soon, and I was going with him this time.

His crew had unloaded more freight than we would be hauling back. There were a few new items, however, and there were also the empty burlap sacks with the words "COFFEE" on some of them, and "TEA" on others. Under these words was the stamp of an anchor. Sometimes when Captain Murphy signed his name, he made the extended part of the letter "y" of his last name in the fashion of an anchor.

Captain Murphy was a close friend of mine and was very perceptive. This time, however, the secrets would remain between my date and me. They would have to remain somewhat a mystery, even to Captain Murphy, though it seemed that he still understood the situation in principle. It appeared that, if he really did know and perceive more than I had mentioned to him, he too kept this secret.

Adventures with Lady Murphy

CHAPTER 1

Getting Focused

The cobblestone streets were starting to become crowded as people began their early morning routine at the marketplace. I loved to go to the marketplace, as I suppose all women do. There were common traits among men, and there were common traits among women. It was probably true with women and men that we generally tend to ignore our own distinctive behaviors to the point where we hardly even realize their existence until something brings them into focus.

Focus, that's what I would try to do. Focusing did seem a bit trifling at the moment, for I was actually more ready to relax. I knew I shouldn't have worn these high-heeled shoes. Another choice of shoes might have been better, but you know us ladies…when it comes to being pretty versus being practical…well, being pretty is quite practical. Men didn't always seem to understand that, but it seemed they secretly liked it that way. It seemed to me that we get our sense of self-worth by taking care of ourselves and being presentable. Perhaps being pretty was a sense of security, for we desired security, and we seemed to be more sociable than men were, or at least I thought so.

There was a little oblong circle of grass in the middle of the cobblestone walkway. In this circle was a small evergreen bush. Near it was a cast iron park bench with wooden slats in it. There were other benches and chairs out in front of the shops, but this particular bench would give me the opportunity to be around the activity and allow me to relax as well. It was still cool and early in the morning, but the crowds were already buzzing, and they would be way into the evening.

Focus…that is what I said I would do, and that's what I would try to do. There was so much activity, and I just absolutely loved it. This bench was nice, too. I sat my shopping bag and my purse down beside me. Opening up my shopping bag, I saw the bottle of perfume I had just bought. This was the newest brand in town, and it smelled lovely. A little spray of perfume on one wrist, a rub of it on the other wrist…a little dab on the finger, and a touch behind both ears. This lifted my spirits.

Now, if I could just find my mirror! Had I left it at the house? Had I loaned it to someone? No, I was certain my mirror was in here—in one of the compartments of this purse. This purse had all types of compartments to help keep me organized, and they were already all full…full of things I needed. I needed to clean it out, but right now just finding the mirror would have helped. Okay, there was the coin purse, the nail file, pencil, tissue, brush, comb, house keys, shopping list, lip balm, hand lotion, perfume, hair pins, and on and on. Four compartments searched, stuff lying out all over the park bench, and still no mirror!

I had just bought this purse last week, and I knew it had a mirror in it. I folded my hands in my lap, and I was somewhat perplexed and agitated. I looked up toward the quaint barbershop in front of me just as…was it…? Could it be him? He walked out, brushed his collar, and stood there a moment longer, brushing his shirtsleeves from a fresh haircut, but with his back turned. Was it even possible this could be him?

This couldn't be…I refused…it couldn't be possible, it couldn't be happening to me. No! I hurried frantically to change inconspicuously into my newest shoes. The ones I had on matched, but not as well as my new ones would. I took one off and had the new one on. The one I had taken off still sat on the ground beside me. He would soon leave, I was sure of it. I crammed all of my stuff back into the disorderly purse, not bothering to latch it. I looked up. He was looking at me.

There I sat with one new shoe on and one old shoe on. One old shoe sat on the ground, and the other new shoe sat on the ground beside it. A bulging purse sat next to me. I immediately thought of the time that we women spend preparing for the grand moment! I guess this was my grand moment! He smiled, looked at his watch, and walked on down the sidewalk. Well, there was no ignoring the scene he had observed. I now know men evidently see the world differently.

At least he was not who I had thought and hoped he was. I would see my date again, Lord willing, in a much more prepared setting, just as we had promised that day at the pier before I had to return on the ship I had arrived on. At any rate, I was not going to sit here looking like this. I put my other new shoe on and straightened up my clothes a little.

I thought again about my mirror. I pulled back the purse flap, and there was the mirror. Sure enough, just as the sales lady had told me, the mirror with this purse was built in. Opening two snaps would display the mirror. Well, my hair hadn't looked as bad as I thought it would, but I guess I did kind of remind myself of a cute little puppy that had just been surprised.

So much for relaxation! I was ready to resume my walk and shopping. I quickly reorganized my purse, and it no longer bulged open. It was amazing what a little order and self-control would do for people and objects.

Let's see…Focus. A new focus, a different way of looking at things, a new start, a fresh new look at some otherwise familiar surroundings…This would do me good. The sun was starting to shine brighter, and it still was a cool day, as well as a great day for shopping.

There were a lot of people walking in the middle of town. Horse-drawn carriages were not generally allowed in the very center of town, although they were allowed to bring deliveries to the back of the shops. The other carriages that lined the street were only the hand-drawn ones that carried the specialty items of the salespeople.

CHAPTER 2

Discussing Things

The atmosphere was one of festivity. Fresh bread baked at the nearby bakery, and a train's steam locomotive hissed at the junction. The windmills, grain elevators, and storage bins were ready for crop storage and processing. Everything seemed to be full of activity this morning.

The open area was fine for walking, but I decided I would rather walk on the wooden sidewalks under the canvas overhangs of the nearby shops. There was the scent of the candle shop, the potpourri and apothecary shop, the woodcraft shop, the flower shop, the candy shop, and the Coffee & Tea Shop. I loved it!

The Coffee & Tea Shop was one of my favorites. The coffee and tea served there was some of the best in the world. I also liked the very elegant service and etiquette of the servers in the shop. Sometimes I could not decide whether it was the coffee blends or the seasoned spice tea that tasted the best. It seemed coffee always won out in terms of the aroma that filled the air. It was enough to draw me into the Coffee & Tea Shop.

It was more properly called the Coffee & Tea Shop, but the locals did not consistently call it that. Sometimes they just called it the beverage house. There was no liquor or tobacco there, which was the case in the rest of town as well. It was instead a very nice, quaint, well-mannered town. Carousers and the ill-mannered were neither welcomed nor allowed. I loved this environment because little children could play without fear, and anyone could walk out of the range of the lanterns at night and not have to worry.

The town watchman spent more time providing directions to visitors, telling people what time it was or if their partner had passed by that way, and getting children's toys off the roof than with any trouble. Sometimes the children had to be led by their parents away from the watchman, for they enjoyed playing around him and listening to his stories of adventure.

Inside the Coffee & Tea Shop were many small tables that normally seated about four people. There were no complaints if someone wanted to combine one or more tables, so this happened quite often. Although certain personalities and interests drew people together, the Coffee & Tea Shop was a place where self-invitation was welcomed. It had been awhile since I had been in, so I was glad to be there again. A person could go in alone, sit down at almost any table, and soon be welcomed into a conversation.

Lanterns lined the walls, and sunshine came in. Perhaps one of the most interesting things in this shop was the large, wind-up carousel. It had colorful ponies and horses circling with a ceramic dog or two in pursuit, birds made of cloth flying overhead, and a built-in music box that played. This carousel was similar in resemblance to the much larger one near the center of the town.

The inside of the shop buzzed with voices. Oh, the subjects to talk about! Who was wearing a new dress, how the flowers were growing, how the children were doing, who was marrying whom, the new wagon, the new house…it was the fellowship that mattered most of all.

I walked toward the counter. On my way, I noticed some very pretty flowers in a planter that lined the wall. They reminded me of some that were growing near Mother and Father's house. As I looked back up, I saw the menu.

Now came the selection time…the decision of whether I wanted coffee or spiced tea. I tossed this thought around in my mind for a short while, and then the coffee won out again. I went ahead to take a seat at a table. The server would be by soon to provide a cup and fill it with coffee. It was really better that way, because trying to walk with a cup full of fresh, hot coffee through a room full of visiting women was similar to a long-tailed cat in a room full of rocking chairs!

As I looked around, I smiled and waved as I saw many familiar faces. Although everybody is friendly at the Coffee & Tea Shop, it is still considered common courtesy to see if your approach is responded to in a welcoming manner. I noticed a table toward the back that had three empty seats. The table had been completely full only moments earlier, but now only Lady Murphy sat there alone. I thought this might be a good time to visit with her.

She had no bonnet on, and her hair was pulled back and fixed with a hair clip. Her dress was modest, with borders of lace. She welcomed me kindly. She had a very favorable reputation. I had no problem understanding why she was called "Lady Murphy," for she had every mannerism of a lady.

"Have a seat," she said, as she pulled out a chair near her. She raised her cup of tea to her lips and said, "It's a gorgeous day outside, isn't it?"

"Oh, lovely," I exclaimed.

Just then, the server rolled the service cart up to our table and poured my cup of coffee. Oh, the wonderful smell of fresh-brewed coffee! It seemed to lift the spirit and bring clarity of perspective and focus.

I observed Lady Murphy for a moment. She seemed to be a very graceful person, and one whose movements and mannerisms portrayed peace and concern for those around her. Perhaps this was the reason she had such a good reputation here. It seems the qualities and mannerisms that a sincere person had (or could acquire) were ones that an insincere person could not successfully fake for very long. No, Lady Murphy was kind and genuine.

I looked outside at the numerous people passing by and coming into this shop. There seemed to be a steady stream of people entering the shop for a moment of relaxation and refreshment before continuing with their day. At that moment, I wondered what I might do with the rest of my day. I was bound by nothing particular, so I didn't have to worry; yet, I wanted to make the most of the day.

Just then Lady Murphy inquired about some new skirts at the stores. That was all it took to snap my imagination into motion. I could see display racks lined with sweaters, display bins full of socks and hosiery, various colors and textures of fabrics, and blouses and dresses. It was as though the lever had been moved into position on a tightly wound music box. I began to talk, and talk, and talk. I talked about this fabric…about that style…this design…about how they fit…about all of the colors. The nice thing about it was that Lady Murphy seemed to enjoy the conversation as much as I did. This subject seemed to be a favorite one for her, too.

We both had our beverages refilled and continued talking. Shoes were also a favorite topic of ours. It reminded me somewhat of the woman mentioned in Proverbs 31 in the King James Version of the Bible who is diligent to shop and prepare things for her family. Perhaps it was just the inherent nature of a woman to want to shop. It had to be done, you know, so what's wrong with enjoying it? At least that's the way I had it figured.

A growl in my stomach made me realize it was near lunchtime. I asked, "Lady Murphy, would you like to have a meal with me at the dining area of my father's inn?"

"Sure, why not?" was her reply. Then she said, "Did I understand you to say that you wanted me to have a meal with you at the dining area of your father's inn?"

I said, "Sure, you heard it right. It's a very nice place."

Lady Murphy was familiar with my father's inn. We paid the server and made our way from the Coffee & Tea Shop.

While we walked Lady Murphy asked, "Why then, if your father has a dining room at his inn, do you stop for your coffee at the Coffee & Tea Shop?"

"Oh, I love the variety and the fellowship," I said.

"I understand," she said.

I began to share some of my thoughts with her. I told her that I traveled often as part of my work as a detective, but that I hoped to settle down soon. You know...at least to get married...maybe start a family. Even then I would like to travel, but only if my husband and I could travel together. Otherwise, I might as well stay single, and I don't want to do that.

"Marriage is a very serious step, but from that gleam in your eye, I don't believe you want to stay single," said Lady Murphy.

"No, I really don't," I said. "I just want to be sure. I've traveled around quite a lot, and I've met a lot of gentlemen. Only a few have seemed special, but there is one a little different—who seems to have really caught my heart. I actually met him at the dining area of my father's inn.

I went on to explain, "Having a father who owns an inn at a seaport gives an advantage to meeting various gentlemen. However, the problem is I often travel, which has made settling into a lasting relationship more difficult. In addition, the men who come into port are often seafaring men that are sailors and merchants and don't necessarily want to settle down to any specific family life. All this seems to show in their mannerisms. Oh, I've seen some men that are very committed to their loved ones and are sailors. I guess it all hinges on finding the right one.

"Maybe I'm really not as ready to settle down as I think I am, and maybe that's the reason why I haven't found the right one yet. However, I really do think that is changing. For instance, the last significant romantic conversation I had with a man was not long ago, even though it seems like it. We had a meal together at one of the tables on the pier.

"You know…the tables with the frilly umbrellas over them? Well, we sat there, and we talked, and we talked more intently than perhaps either of us had talked to anyone else before. I think we were both a little shocked, yet excited, too, that we seemed to have such common thoughts about so many things. In fact, it was almost like I could start a sentence, and he could finish it. Without a spoken word, a glance or mannerism seemed to convey understanding between us. It was so special.

"It was as if we had grown up together or had spent a lot of time around each other in the past. When it was time for me to leave, I found myself actually wanting to stay and continue talking with him. I certainly wished I could have at least stayed longer. Instead, I had to go, but we did promise to keep in touch.

"The only problem, or at least one problem, is that we both have had to travel since then. We have had to rely on trying to contact each other through mail or messages conveyed by word-of-mouth to someone who would actually be going to the port where the other could get the message. Otherwise, we can only wonder, and that is what we both have had to do.

"I have had to wonder if he really cared for me like he said he did. I have wondered if he was happy. I have wondered if he even thinks of me, or if he has found some new love. I have also wondered if he is still trying to get in touch with me. It seems there is at least more confidence and reassurance if a person is actually married to someone. At least they seem to have a more significant pledge and statement of commitment than people who are just dating or who are just friends.

"All of these things have caused me to consider marriage more than I think I ever have in the past. In the past, it was more an idea I entertained as an event that would take place someday, somewhere out there, in the distant future. Then, all of a sudden, it did not seem to be a thought that was so far out there.

"I was actually a little shocked when I realized how significant my friendship with him had become. I then realized how much one personality could lean on another to the point it seemed like the two personalities were actually only one. I realized that continuing along a path such as that could easily lead to marriage before a person even thought to protest it. However, I would not protest it, if that should be, although I am a little concerned about the seriousness of commitment and about my fear of being hurt if the relationship doesn't develop.

"Love is probably about as close to magnificence as anything a human can get. A man and woman meet, and sometimes without them even knowing, a romance starts. It is as though their hearts are already aware. They seem to become extensions of one another, while a mutual fondness for each other draws them together. As more and more mutual feelings and interests become shared, these emotions and feelings intertwine like vines, and so love seems to grow."

"I agree," said Lady Murphy.

All of a sudden, I realized I had been talking nonstop! I looked over at Lady Murphy and smiled.

She smiled back, as if reading my mind, and said, "You need not explain. I fully understand. Love is a subject worth talking about, and it sure beats a lot of other subjects. It can be one of the most exciting and yet one of the most confusing emotions for anyone to deal with. It is not always easy to think about it logically, because the heart is often already involved."

CHAPTER 3

Thinking It Over

"This way," I said, as we turned left down a rock road closer to the pier. I pondered in my mind how carried away I had been, talking about myself and about the idea of love. I thought that perhaps I should apologize for having talked so much about it, but then figured an apology might continue what was already an exhausted subject. To my surprise, Lady Murphy opened the subject again.

She said, "You know, when you look at a man, you might be thinking about romance, or perhaps not. It does seem that when the time is right for dating or romance, it happens in at least one of three ways, though these are not necessarily the only ways. I've seen ladies that were independent and somewhat spicy who proclaimed they weren't even interested in dating or marriage. Next thing you know, they are seeing a particular man regularly, then more regularly, and then they are planning a wedding. So much for their lack of interest in the subject!

"Other ladies seem to be so infatuated by the idea of love and romance that it would appear a million good men could pass by and not one of them would have any attractive advantage over the other. These types of ladies are in love to the point of being oblivious to the fact these men are not all the same, and that the selection of one means forfeiting the others. These kinds of ladies sometimes just marry and then only rethink their choice after they have married. Only then do they sometimes realize they did not truly follow what they felt in their hearts.

"The third type of lady is the one that knows how she feels about marriage and its responsibilities and knows what type of man would be right for the marriage. For her, there is danger she could marry someone she thinks is best at the moment, only to find out differently later. However, most ladies of this third type have already been through the scenarios of the first two types of ladies and have been fortunate enough not to have already married someone.

It is certainly best not to rush into marriage until one's mind is settled on the choice. Marriage is simply not something to enter into without a lot of prayer and honest, objective evaluation."

"Right," I said, agreeing with and appreciating the value of what she was saying. "I guess those first two types of scenarios could be endured at different times, or even at the same time. Yet, a balanced decision about the desire to marry and whom to marry should be made before marriage. Marriage is not for everyone, and some people seem happier unmarried. As I look at my life, where it is going, and what my goals and desires are, I really think marriage is in my future, and that each day is bringing me closer to that moment."

We passed the sun-bleached wooden shrimp shacks with the rusty tin roofs that were on large rocks near the shoreline. Just then, our feet touched the gray wooden boards of the pier. The dining room of my father's inn was just at the other end. If it were not for the fact that my father and mother were there, I suppose I could allow myself to become somewhat lonely at this pier. Here was where I had met the man I think I love, and I intended to meet him again.

Lady Murphy and I found a nearby table and immediately sat down. It had been a pleasant but lengthy walk from the Coffee & Tea Shop to here, and we were both glad to sit down and rest.

I told Lady Murphy to keep our places, and I went and placed our orders. We both wanted a hearty meal of fresh boiled lobster dipped in butter sauce with fried shrimp on the side. I went over and placed our order.

Father commented that I was certainly eating more than my share these days. He raised his eyebrows and gave me an inquisitive sideways glance, as if to inquire, "Who is the other person?"

"It's Lady Murphy. She and I shared coffee and tea earlier this morning, and we are teaming up to do some shopping after we eat," I answered. I lingered around the counter and waited on our meals for a while.

I looked out toward the same cast-iron chairs and table with the umbrella over it where my date and I had made our promise that we would meet again. I hadn't even heard from him. The supply train had brought many things in by rail, the crops had turned out good, and the grain elevators were filled. The windmills and gristmills had been very useful. However, there had not been as many ships in and out of the port, except for the daily runs of the lobster, shrimp, and various fishing boats. When would I see my date again? When would I ever hear from him again?

Father came out with the meals.

"Shall I help you?" he asked when he saw me.

"No, I'll make two trips. Go ahead and help the other customers," I said. Thankfully, the inn was usually a busy place.

I made my way out to the table. As I approached, Lady Murphy was sitting sideways in her chair, turned away from the table and looking out to sea. She saw me approaching and was surprised my hands were so full.

"Let me help," she exclaimed.

She helped place the food on the table, but I assured her there was no need for her to return with me to get the rest of it.

Our meal was delightful and very welcomed right now. Lady Murphy talked more this time. She talked about how she loved the sea.

"The sea seems to have personality," she exclaimed. "One might imagine it has a mind of its own and holds many of the mysteries of the world in its confidence. A person can think of it as though it is some type of imaginary large pool of secrets where a lot of hidden questions, as well as answers are stored. Where there is one person with a question on one shore, and another person who holds the answer on another shore. It doesn't matter how close or how far apart those people might be. Sometimes they are both aware of each other's thoughts or feelings, and express that. Others know something but do not express it. Others simply wonder and wait, hoping for their ship to come in, as the saying goes.

"The sea seems to provide a sense of freedom, which allows a person to dream without being distracted by many physical objects. Above it is the sky, which has few objects to distract a person. Even things like a sea gull, a star, a cloud, or the sun seem to encourage freedom, imagination, meditation, and prayer."

"That is exactly how I feel about it, although I'm not sure I could have expressed it just that way," I said to Lady Murphy.

"This is excellent lobster. Some of the finest I've ever tasted," she said.

"Great! Then would you like to also eat here tomorrow?" I asked.

"That would work out just fine, I believe," said Lady Murphy.

I was glad she said yes. This was great. Even before we had finished our meal today, we had planned one for tomorrow. This suggested our friendship was mutual, growing, and would continue.

We wasted no time eating our meals, as shopping was still very fresh on our minds. Luckily, the clothing stores were not far away.

The fisheries nearby, along with the eateries, kept the crows, pigeons, sea gulls, cats, and dogs well-fed. The cats tended to stay away from the water, though they seemed to love the scraps of fish. The crows, pigeons, and sea gulls frequently lighted on rocks, ledges, and pier beams farther out. Once in a while a crow, pigeon, or sea gull would move in closer and snatch a goody from a nearby trash box or unattended table. I remember my date had said crows were interesting birds. Oh, I wish he were here!

The dogs seemed to stay around the shops and eateries more for the leftover food. Every now and then, there would be a little extra commotion. Either a dog or a cat would harass the other, and the chase would begin, and the people they excited would follow behind them. The dog usually got the blame, but a person sometimes had to wonder if the cat didn't harass the dog in the first place. Maybe the cat and the dog enjoyed having little boys and girls hollering and running after them. That often got the adults involved in the chase, too. It suddenly made for a very lively scene.

Lady Murphy and I finished our meals and headed toward the nearby clothing stores. There were many nice shops along the way. There were also discount shops, offering the same quality of clothes as the nice shops. The discount shops reduced prices because the clothes had not yet been packaged or displayed as nicely. The discount shops were the places I went to shop for bargains. I visited the more elegant shops for ideas and a great atmosphere while browsing, or when I needed a specialty item or guarantee.

Today was a day for sightseeing and window-shopping. We did more looking and visiting than anything else. A new shipment of clothing and other articles was due into port soon, so we both decided to wait, even though we saw many nice things to buy. Our shopping took us to the nearby general store. There was seldom a time when there wasn't some item needed from there.

In the general store, there was a large pottery room. There were finished products and items freshly made by the potter. It was interesting and instructive to see how a piece of clay, moistened a little bit, became a beautiful and useful vessel.

My mind reflected upon the time mentioned in the King James Version of the Bible in Jeremiah 18:1–6 where the Spirit of God spoke to the prophet Jeremiah, instructing him to go down to the potter's house where he would hear more from God. I watched in the pottery room as the clay spun on the potter's wheel and pressure was applied, at times upon the inside and at times upon the outside. I thought about how the clay would later be placed in the fire and tested, and then there would be the finished product.

Our life in the hand of God could seem that way. According to Genesis 2:7, man was first a piece of dust of the earth, formed and fashioned in the hands of the Creator. Pressures come to us from within and without, but through the caring hands of our Creator, we, too, can become a useful vessel to Him. I was determined to obey my Creator and remain confident that, regardless of any inner or outer tests or pressures I might face in life, I would let God's will fashion my life.

I noticed that Lady Murphy had found a teapot she decided to buy. About the same time, I saw two thick coffee cups. I also saw teacups, but a person could just as easily have said coffee cups or teacups. It was interesting, how we identified the container by what beverage was in it. I couldn't help but think how the Bible mentions that our bodies are the temples of God, as it is written in I Corinthians 3:16–17. The Bible indicates in Acts chapter 2 and Romans 8:5–9 that it is mandatory that we be filled with God's spirit in order to please God.

A vessel is often referred to by what it has within, as seems to be indicated in I Corinthians 10:21. I also reflected on how much care a potter takes to fashion a vessel into what they want it to be. It is important for us to keep our outward appearance in such a manner that is pleasing to God's design and instruction and which reflects outwardly the Spirit of God within, as is referred to in Matthew 23:26–27. Ironically, Lady Murphy and I had both chosen to buy the plain clay vessels.

CHAPTER 4

Like a Child

The sun was starting to set, and the outside lanterns were being lit. It was not yet dark but soon would be. The streetlamps would light the walk along the way, and it would be a pleasant walk.

As we left the general store, a horse-drawn carriage pulled up. With a quick glance at each other, it was decided. Soon there was the sound of horse hooves on the pavement and the sound of carriage wheels underneath us. This beat walking at this time of the evening, and we could be talking rather than watching where we were going.

I reached my destination first, and Lady Murphy had only a short distance left to go. I paid my fare, and exited the carriage. We exchanged good evenings and agreed to have lunch together again tomorrow at the dining area of my father's inn.

While at home that evening, I thought about the events of the day and, particularly, about my friendship with Lady Murphy. She had been so understanding and kind when I had rambled on about my date and my future. She not only listened, but also actually offered some wise advice on the matter afterward.

I pondered whether she liked me because she enjoyed helping people, such as myself, with decisions. I also considered whether she liked me because we shared common interests, such as shopping and dining. Had she noticed some potential in me and wanted to be a friendly mentor to see those qualities develop in me?

I noticed that though Lady Murphy was elegant, she was not fragile. Though she liked dressing up in nice clothes, she also wore casual or work clothes for other occasions. I admired this trait about her. She was certainly a respected and polished lady, and someone from whom I could definitely learn. It could be that providence had put us on the same path for a while. Perhaps we had both learned something from each other. We at least shared a friendship and planned to visit again tomorrow.

The next morning was cool and refreshing but with a nice touch of sunshine. Mother and Father had already left for the inn. I had rested well but had gone to sleep late last night.

I stepped out on the front porch of my mother and father's place. My dog came up to visit. He is a friendly dog. Although there are chickens, roosters, ducks, goats, cows, horses, and donkeys around here, his ears rose a little when he looked out to the field and saw the crows. The birds and the squirrels seem particularly busy today. Perhaps it is because of this nice weather.

I had recently been pondering many things in my life while sipping a cup of coffee. Some people have said coffee can keep you awake, but I think a busy mind will keep you awake, coffee or not. I had been thinking about one of my most recent cases. The case seemed to come to me by chance, right here in this local area.

There had been two little girls in town with their mother. They walked into the fabric store. The girls started playing hide-and-seek among the fabric. Soon, without a new place to hide from each other, they decided to hide from their mother. They hid under the clothes rack, then ran out the door, jumped off the porch, and climbed quickly into a horse-drawn wagon parked nearby.

They were under the covering and lying quietly when, all of a sudden, the wagon began to jolt and move. They looked at each other, then peeked out of the back of the wagon, but could see no one, only woods and the back of the fabric store.

Knowing they would be in trouble, they were too scared to scream and too scared to jump out. They knew their mother would correct them for leaving the store, and the driver of the wagon would not be happy. They hid themselves even lower among the stuff.

The older of the two would occasionally rise up to check their surroundings and to assure her sister she could remember the way back. She really thought she could, but everything seemed to keep changing.

Then the wagon stopped almost as abruptly as it had started. "Shush," they whispered and hid again. If the driver of the wagon found out they were in there without asking, they would be in trouble, and he would tell their mother. If they ran real fast, they might be able to get back to the store before their mother even missed them.

They heard a rustling noise around the front of the wagon. The wagon rocked a little, and then things were pretty quiet. There was a sound of a barn door or something opening a short distance away. They believed the man had parked the wagon outside and went inside the barn. Now was the time to escape!

Climbing out the back of the wagon and dropping to the ground seemed like a long drop, but they had done stuff like this before. The main thing was to get out of there and back to the fabric store before their mother noticed they were gone.

The man told me later that while he was still inside the barn, he had heard a small commotion out by the wagon and the muffled sound of a dog barking. Thinking it was usual for the dog to chase a rabbit or some other animal, he paid it no attention.

The dog, evidently wanting excitement and someone to play with, took out after the girls. They ran down the road with the dog following them. They could scarcely keep from screaming. They left the road for a clump of bushes, hoping to lose the dog and slow down. It didn't work. The dog put his nose to the ground and started to run around in a circle with his tail wagging. He started trying to track the girls.

The man finished picking up the tools he needed from inside the barn and walked outside where he had parked the wagon. He looked back down the road and saw the dog with his nose to the ground, running around as if hunting something. The man called the dog, never seeing the girls. They watched, giggling, as the dog went back and followed behind the wagon when it started down the road in the direction away from them.

The girls waited until the wagon and the dog were out of sight before getting out onto the road again. Heading back in the direction they had come, they ran and then they walked, but the road seemed longer and longer. The sun continued to get lower and lower in the sky.

Just then, another dog came out of the woods to greet them. It was my dog, and he was friendly. A neighbor up the road had five dogs, but those dogs only barked at the girls. My dog did not bark nor chase them, so the girls and my dog walked together for some ways until the girls were tired and wanted to rest.

I was on my way back from town that evening and had rounded the corner near a large barn when my dog started barking and I noticed the girls. "Hello," I said. "What brings you two out here? Where are your parents?" I asked.

The oldest of the girls said, "Oh, we are out walking, but this is a long road and we're hungry, so we sat down to rest. We were with Mother in town shopping today, so we started playing. We hid from her and rode out here in the back of a wagon, but trying to walk back is a very long way."

"I should say so," I responded. "Especially since you are both so young, and it is getting so late. Don't you think your mother is worried about you right now?" I asked.

"She might not be worried since she doesn't know we are out here," said the oldest girl.

"Well then," I said, "if you were shopping with your mother today and then rode in a wagon out here, and now you are walking back this late in the evening, and your mother doesn't know you're out here, I imagine she is getting very concerned about you."

The oldest of the girls said, "We were hurrying back as quickly as we could. It's just been a long walk. We didn't mean to come out so far. We thought the wagon would stop soon, but nobody knew we were in there."

The youngest girl then said, "We were playing hide-and-seek and hid in the wagon from Mother. I want Mother."

"So you girls are lost, and nobody but me knows you are way out here," I said. "Let's start with who you are and where you live."

The older girl told the younger one, "I think you got us in trouble."

I interrupted the older girl and again asked their names and where they lived. They then began to tell me the whole story.

Soon my mother came around the corner in the carriage. Mother said, "Well, well, what have we here? Looks like you two are the pretty little girls whose mother has been looking for them. Let's make a deal. Why don't you two just hop in this carriage with me, and I will give you a ride back into town to see your mother."

The girls looked at me for assurance, and then I helped them into the carriage. My dog followed the three of them in the carriage for a while and then ran up to follow me. They weren't far from town, but I knew their mother was bound to be worried.

I was involved in detective work and traveled quite a bit. Being a detective required skill and diplomacy. I guess, in a sense, parents at times have to be detectives, like the time I hid under the wash pot from my father.

I could hear my father calling for me. I would giggle each time I heard him call. Then I heard him and Mother walk past. Father was saying, "Well, without a little girl around here anymore, I guess I'll save my money and won't buy that candy the next time I go into town."

"Here I am," I yelled. What was life for if there weren't any treats now and then?

I didn't always manage so easily, though. Like the Easter Sunday when I had my Easter dress and new socks on, but no shoes. Mother was fixing my hair, combing it this way and that way. She told me to stay right there until she got back. She went to do something, and I ran outside.

Unluckily for me, the rain the night before had made a mud puddle just outside the back door. I almost had my sock washed clean when Mother came out the door. I wanted to run, but knew I was in trouble. I got a whipping right then and there. Then, when I got back from church that day, I had to sit in the corner for a while. I understand it all now, but at the time, it seemed I would have to spend my whole life alone in that corner.

My dog on the porch stirred a little near the chair I was sitting in when he saw a squirrel scurry up a tree. That brought my thoughts back to the present. I realized I had been daydreaming. I was supposed to meet Lady Murphy in town today. I was already dressed somewhat casually for the day. I rushed in to see the time on the grandfather clock just before it chimed a half past eleven in the morning. It was time to get into town if I was going to meet Lady Murphy at mealtime.

Today I decided that I would wear shoes without heels. I knew Lady Murphy and I would likely walk quite a bit. It was not that far into town from here, and today was another nice day for walking. Oh, I had better hurry. I was out the door in no time, headed for town. I arrived rather quickly, having resisted the desire to stop at a shop or two along the way.

As I walked into town, I noticed one or two of the shops appeared to be in rather unusual order. Things that would normally be sitting inside were sitting outside on the porches, with some items even out in the street. I saw no banners indicating any special sale or anything. Surely, they weren't just rearranging the store for cleaning, especially since these were such big items that were sitting out.

As I approached the inn, there was a lot of activity. Everything seemed basically normal, except for the increased amount of people. Crowds of people were walking, talking, laughing, and carrying on in the usual way.

I arrived at the dining area of my father's inn, and entered through the back door of the kitchen. There was Father. He made no comment of anything unusual in town. He did ask me to write down two things on a note since I was there.

"Make a note so that I'll remember to get coffee and tea," he said.

I wrote a note for him, and then asked if he needed my help with anything else.

"No, not at this time," he said.

I went out through the back part of the kitchen to avoid going past the ovens.

CHAPTER 5

Activities in Town

Once outside, I made my way around the side of the inn and out onto the pier. There were more men in town today, and the wagons with their teams of horses were set in closer than usual. Well, it sure seemed a little unusual, but whatever it was, it seemed not to bother anyone.

I glanced around the pier a bit to try to locate Lady Murphy. It was noon, and Lady Murphy and I had agreed to meet here for a meal together. One thing I knew, or at least thought I knew, was that Lady Murphy would be on time and be faithful to her commitment unless something very unexpected or unusual caused her to change her plans.

The way everything seemed today, perhaps there really was something rather unusual going on, and Lady Murphy's plans to meet me here were changed. Maybe she had changed her mind. We women do that, you know. Still it did not seem like Lady Murphy's nature to just abandon her plans without giving a reason.

I stepped forward and began to walk alongside the inn dining room again, this time planning to look inside. Perhaps Lady Murphy decided to wait for me in there. As I walked, I wondered if I had told her a different time to meet. Just then, a tap on my shoulder let me know. I turned around to see Lady Murphy standing there, smiling.

"I saw you standing there. I've been watching you for a short while," Lady Murphy said. "I would have come over sooner, but you appeared as though you had some other small matter to attend to before you came over."

"Well, since we're already both here, close to the inn dining room, let's go ahead and place our order," I said. "I'll go in and tell Father."

"And I'll go ahead and get us a seat, or I can stay around and help you with the food," said Lady Murphy.

"I'll get the food. Go ahead and find us a seat. Father's inn looks busier than normal today, so it might be just a little bit longer before the food is ready anyway," I said.

Lady Murphy made her way out to the tables. Most of the men tended to crowd around the larger, heavier wooden tables, and some of them even sat along the rocks near the pier, tossing out food scraps to the sea gulls, which quickly swooped down for the meal. The more delicate and classy cast-iron tables with the canvas umbrellas over them were readily available. That is where Lady Murphy chose.

The food was not quite ready, but at least I placed our order. Father asked that I come back up to the kitchen in just a minute, as the food should be ready. The smell of fresh-brewed coffee and fresh-cooked food was all it took for me to realize how hungry I really was. "I could eat a basket full of fresh fried shrimp," I said to myself in an exaggerated whisper.

It was good we arrived when we did, because as I made my way onto the pier, more and more people were looking for tables to sit at. I soon saw Lady Murphy with her hand raised, modestly waving at me. There she was. I sat down in the chair across from her, explaining to her that the food should be ready soon.

Lady Murphy began looking in her purse for something. Soon, she pulled out a small list. I asked her if things seemed to be slightly different today since the place was crowded with more people than normal. In addition, the store-owners seemed to be adjusting their merchandise.

Lady Murphy said, "There's a shipment of coffee and tea expected to arrive into port today."

I said, "Do you mean from Captain Murphy?"

"Yes," said Lady Murphy.

I looked at Lady Murphy, observing her when she mentioned Captain Murphy. It seemed obvious that she was very committed to him and that she loved him very much. Though she was married to him, she wore no wedding ring. A wedding ring apparently didn't really indicate whether a person was married or not. Some people wore them, and they were not even married. Other people didn't wear them because of religious reasons, and Lady Murphy certainly seemed to be religious.

"I had better go see if the food is ready," I said to Lady Murphy.

"Wait, I'll go with you," said Lady Murphy.

"No, no. I can get the food or have one of the waitresses help me if I need help. Stay here so we don't lose our spot at the table. It's no problem, and my compliment," I said. Lady Murphy conceded, so I went to get the food. Sure enough, it was ready. Father was very busy, so I couldn't talk with him much.

I did get a waitress to help me carry the food out to the table. We prayed over our food and then began talking. We both wanted to go shopping. Lady Murphy suggested we wait until after Captain Murphy's ship came in, which she said should be into port soon. She gave two reasons to wait for the new arrival. One was the obvious fact that more goods would be available. The second fact was that the stores were willing to sell some items at a discount if you bought them before the store arranged them on the shelf.

"In fact," she said, "some stores send their own wagons to the pier, and as soon as the freight is unloaded from the ship, they will deal right then and there. This, though, is usually more likely to happen with the very large items. Otherwise, the scene gets too congested. Most of the smaller items are carried in crates to the stores and distributed there. With the larger items, almost everybody is happier if they can reach their final customer as soon as the merchandise is unloaded from the ship."

I liked shopping, and I liked Lady Murphy. She didn't just shop; she had a plan of action—a strategy! She even had a list of what items had been ordered and which stores had ordered them. That seemed easy enough, I guess, if you had the right connections. A person could know before the ship was sent out what items had been ordered and by whom. Whether the items actually arrived was another story. According to Lady Murphy, we should soon know that, too.

As she looked out to sea, she pointed. There, coming into port, but still a ways out, was Captain Murphy's black ship with midnight blue sails.

I almost wanted to cry. Could it be there was a letter on this ship? This was the pier where my date and I had made our promises that we would meet again in the future. The only problem was that with both of us traveling, we hadn't been able to send a letter back and forth. We had been unable to nail down the specific time to meet again. Since voyage ships had not been traveling to common parts, it had been difficult to send a letter. I would be sure to try to send a letter out this time.

"Will there be mail on this ship?" I asked hopefully.

Lady Murphy replied, "Yes, most likely. Usually there is mail. It is usually the very first thing unloaded. It is actually lowered over the side, down to the pier, and onto the mail wagon even before the ramp is put down to unload any other freight.

"The postal workers rush it immediately to the post office and begin sorting it out. They rush as quickly as they can, but, depending on the amount of mail, they don't always get it put out like normal, so they most often stay open almost until midnight so people can get their mail. You know the excitement and anticipation. It's like watching children with new toys."

Lady Murphy said, "I have a plan. Do you want to meet the ship?"

I said, "No, I wish I did, but there is a very remote chance I might have a letter."

Lady Murphy said, "Okay, I suggest we split up as a plan of action to do our shopping. I will meet the ship as it arrives. It is almost against the pier now. You go over to the general store. The general store ordered some elegant vases, and I would love to have one. Here is some money to cover the cost.

"I should be able to meet you within one hour after you arrive there. The general store often pays extra to get their wash pots and vases unloaded right after the mail. If they have received the vases, they will most likely know which ones you are seeking. I prefer the midnight blue vases, but I will accept any color if the midnight blue ones are not available. The mail should later be sorted and ready, and we will already have the vase and any other items you might see."

I agreed with her plan and rushed on, not slowing as she prepared to meet the ship. It was like two young children playing as if they were very, very important people on a very, very important mission! In seconds, I was out of Lady Murphy's sight. The crowd that had been lazily lingering around the pier moved collectively toward the arriving ship. Mostly men, wagons, and teams of horses moved forward, all eager and ready to unload their merchandise.

As I hurried to the general store, I began to think more, or really, hope more, about the possibility of a letter arriving on that ship. It really was a stretch of hope. However, a little hope would add to the excitement and romanticism of it all, and I was certain I would send out a letter of my own. Come to think of it, though, I hadn't so much as asked Lady Murphy when Captain Murphy's ship would set sail from the harbor again or where it would be going after that.

Oh well, one way or the other, I intended to get a letter to my date. Even if I had to put a letter in a bottle and throw it into the sea and hope it would arrive at the correct place on a distant shore. I was desperate enough to tie it to the leg of a sea gull or a crow and see if it carried it to him.

My thoughts humored me, as I was being a little fanciful in my ideas. It was all in good fun, and I knew the foolishness of it, but I was still determined. In addition, I wasn't even very certain I really liked this man that much…or so I told myself. Perhaps it was the mystery, the curiosity, and the excitement of discovering whether this man might turn out to be different from any other. Then again, I think I really knew.

I arrived at the general store, but the wagon of freight had not arrived yet. I decided not to chance missing the delivery just because a wagon was not there yet. Perhaps they had not ordered a whole wagonload. Perhaps there was not more than one burlap sack full, and it was possible to place that across the back of a horse or mule.

As a wagon drew near and slowed down close to the general store, it seemed my question was about to be answered. I asked the store attendant, who was standing on the porch looking toward the arriving wagon, "Do you have the midnight blue vases?"

"I don't know yet, ma'am. We'll both have to wait and see what actually arrives. It's only one part to order something, but it's another part to receive it," the store attendant answered.

"Yes, I guess I am being a little too quick," I said, laughing.

After the wagon driver had a chance to open the crate, the store attendant then asked if the load of vases had arrived.

"Yes, big midnight blue vases in perfect condition," said the wagon driver.

I then asked them how much the vases were. The wagon driver and the store attendant looked at a shopping invoice, added a few things, and named their price.

"The wagon driver says you can take another fifteen percent off if you take the vase right off the wagon," said the store attendant.

I made the deal. The wagon driver and store attendant started unloading the other freight. The wagon driver showed me the area of the crate where the vases were. I dove in to find them. "Oh, my! Are these the vases?" I asked the wagon driver.

"Yes, ma'am," he replied as he passed with an armload of stuff.

CHAPTER 6

What an Arrangement!

The vases were large! They were more like wash pots! I was shocked at the size and shocked that Lady Murphy had sent me over by myself to pick one up. Wait, I reasoned to myself, Lady Murphy only said to rush over here to make the deal, and she should be able to meet me within one hour from the time I arrived here.

While I thought about that, Lady Murphy arrived pulling a hand-drawn wagon. She was dressed in very plain and casual clothes. Wow! We really were acting more like little girls than like adults, but what fun it was! Up the loading ramp came Lady Murphy. In no time, the two of us had the large vase on the hand-drawn wagon. Down the ramp and up the road we went.

Soon, we were stopping at a shed near the side of the Murphy's large house.

"Let's put it right in here," said Lady Murphy.

I didn't question her, but I was wondering why she chose this temporary spot when I was here to help her unload it.

"Right here," she said, as she positioned the hand-drawn wagon with the vase still on it inside the shed. "Okay, let's start at the park bench under the lamppost there in the town square, and from there we can hurry through the stores and shop, shop, shop!" said Lady Murphy, squealing with excitement.

I was almost squealing with excitement, too. We were definitely behaving like two small girls, except we were both grownups. And shop, we did! All kinds of new items were in the stores now.

After we had made a day of it, Lady Murphy suggested we eat again at the dining area of Father's inn. We both agreed that some time to put away our belongings and refresh ourselves was the thing to do. Our meeting place would be back at the dining area of Father's inn this evening.

I had actually bought numerous things today and at a good buyer's price. I decided to dress rather nicely for the evening, just because. I guess it was just part of being a woman to want to dress up now and then.

I met Lady Murphy near my father's inn dining room, and she was already there and waiting. She was usually on time unless there was some reason to be late.

As I approached her, she said, "I'd like to buy our meals tonight."

I nicely objected to this, saying it was a small matter and one that my father didn't mind now and then.

She said, "Well, there has been an unexpected change in our meal plans."

I asked, "Would another time better?"

Lady Murphy replied, "Oh, no, we should be able to keep our plans like we talked about. I just wondered if you might object to a few other people joining us?"

"How many shall I go place the orders for then?" I asked.

"Are you sure you won't mind having guests?" she asked.

"I won't mind at all," I said.

Lady Murphy said, "I really don't know what they would prefer to have. Why don't we wait a minute or two? They should be here any moment. Let's sit down on this bench and wait."

We sat there, and then I looked down and began straightening my shoe.

I heard a male voice ask, "Ready to share a meal together, Lady Murphy?"

"I sure am," I heard her say.

When I looked up, I was startled! My mouth fell open, and I could not believe my eyes nor withhold my excitement. There stood the good-looking man in crisp clothes, Captain Murphy, and alongside him, at this very pier, was the very man I had pledged I would meet with again! He and I were both ecstatic!

Lady Murphy asked, with a twinkle in her eye and a slight smile, "Have you two met before?" The answer seemed so obvious that I didn't bother to answer.

Captain Murphy suggested we all go ahead and place our orders.

Lady Murphy said, "There are two cast-iron tables with canvas umbrellas over them near the edge of the pier. I already have them reserved. Your father and mother will be out any minute to join us. I think we all have a lot of visiting to do."

Something led me to believe that Captain Murphy and Lady Murphy knew more than I thought about this situation.

My date looked over at me at this moment, smiled, and said, "I am not sure we could have planned for any better arrangement than this."

I smiled back and said, "Perhaps it is just providential that it has happened this way. Sometimes it seems we arrive at places in life where we seem to be the ones most surprised."

"Would you two like to join us?" Lady Murphy asked from near the table.

With a smile and a glance at each other, the silent yes was understood.

THE END OF BOOK ONE.

978-0-595-34019-4
0-595-34019-9

Printed in the United States
107417LV00003B/352-369/A